Explicit Instruction

Jamie Jones

ISBN-10: 1-947208-13-6

ISBN-13: 978-1-947208-13-1

2ND EDITION

A Note to the Reader

This edition of Explicit Instruction is a complete revision from the first edition. The original work was published in 2014.

A Note to the Reader

This edition of Explicit Instruction is a complete revision from the first edition. The original work was published in 2014.

CHAPTER ONE

Appointments were a pain in the ass. Nikki Dayton didn't make a habit of being on time. It was hot, she was tired, and on top of that, she ran late. She'd worked a full shift at the restaurant and had gotten the latest appointment she could with her advisor. Meeting with that woman today was crucial, as she'd procrastinated long enough. Damn, this was when Nikki would get her student teaching assignment. The last major hurdle toward finishing her program and earning her degree.

Her car snaked along the winding road to Arcadia College. She had a four o'clock appointment and the dashboard clock displayed four forty-five. Her advisor would probably blow a gasket if her car didn't first. The old workhorse had served her well since she was sixteen. Five years later, it still sputtered along.

Double shifts at the restaurant had paid for college, and she wasn't about to blow it now. As she maneuvered her car around the last bend, she hoped her advisor would still be there. Then it happened.

The car stopped, and Nikki froze. There wasn't any kind of a pop, so she couldn't have a blowout. Besides, that wouldn't have made the car stop. The engine had cut off. She turned the key in the ignition and nothing happened.

Why does this always happen to me?

She stepped out of her Toyota Camry and walked around the car. Unfortunately, she knew little of cars, so she really didn't know what she was looking for. A few cars passed her but didn't stop. Then again, she hadn't turned on her emergency lights.

Is this an emergency?

Nikki clenched her fists and squinted in the bright Louisiana sunshine. Spending five minutes in the sun usually resulted in her freckled skin turning lobster red. She rummaged through her purse for the sunscreen.

Her advisor probably thought she'd flaked. This assignment meant everything to Nikki, and she was about to be even more delayed.

Damn. Why had she waited so long? Because she never turned down a shift at the restaurant, that's why. Go to class. Go to work. That had been her routine for several years, going into this fourth and last year.

She kicked a few pebbles and ran a hand through her naturally red hair. The air smelled of dust and freshly cut grass. Not the best combination.

That appointment was the key to her future. She'd walk up the damned drive and leave her crappy old junk heap here.

A hip-hop song blasted from somewhere down the road,

drowning out any other sounds. Not a new tune, but some OG classic from long ago. Within a hot minute, a shiny, spotless, San Marino Blue BMW crawled to a stop right by her.

"Need a lift?" The young man wore shades concealing his eyes, but he sported a bright smile and a silky voice.

"No," Nikki answered perhaps too quickly. But it was true. She didn't need a lift. She needed help getting her car started.

"What's wrong?"

Nikki frowned. Would she be standing by the road if she could tell him what's wrong? She shrugged.

"Can I take a look?"

Nikki took a look at *him*. A young black man, lean, muscular arms, thug-brother-from-the-hood kinda look. His smile featured a sparkling gold grill, and he wore a green cap with a matching green and white shirt.

"Sure," Nikki said. She probably would have turned him down had it not been for her advisory appointment.

The sinewy young man stepped out of the car. She could practically catch a whiff of the new car smell. He was tall, towering over her. His green and white shorts and matching athletic shoes were perfectly clean. The only thing missing from the image he tried to project was the bling.

"Pop the hood."

Nikki hesitated. Hadn't he figured out she knew nothing of cars? His lanky arm reached through the open window and pulled something. The hood popped open, and he disappeared under it. When Nikki took a few steps toward the front of her vehicle, she was greeted with a view of his perfectly round buttocks.

She shifted her weight from one foot to the other. Heat surged through her core, and it had nothing to do with the late-summer temperature. This wasn't time to think about a young man's buns. What she needed to focus on was the important advisory meeting—a meeting that she'd missed.

"Found it. You got a wrench?"

Nikki raised her arms, palms up. The young man nodded, went to his car, and returned with the needed tool. He was back under the hood for less than a minute before he emerged.

"You're good to go."

He looks so good I'll go with him anywhere.

"What was it?"

"Loose connection on your battery. I tightened it, but you should have a professional look at it next time you take your car in. It'll hold for a while, but it looked corroded, so I'd say it needs to be replaced." He hadn't gotten so much of a spot of grease on him. Those designer duds remained pristine.

Nikki nodded. "Thank you."

"You're welcome. Start her up." The young man gestured to her car.

She was the one all started up. A tingling ran through her core and her cheeks burned. But why? He wasn't even remotely her type.

I don't have a type, actually.

Nikki suppressed a smile and got into her car. She turned the key, and it started right up.

"Thanks again." She avoided his gaze, certain she'd blush.

"You're welcome again, miss…"

Nikki waved at him. "I appreciate your help." She stepped on the gas.

He's cute.

He had a sweet smile and the body of an athlete. Well spoken. Well mannered. That contrasted with his manufactured image. Or perhaps that was his style. But the young man was fine.

She pulled her car into the lot. Had she seen him on campus before? No, doubtful. Most of her classes were in the morning. Since he had driven up a few minutes ago, he might have late classes.

Nikki hurried into the education building and squeezed into an elevator. Her advisor was on the second floor, but for some dumb reason, she didn't take the stairs. So now she had to wait for the lethargic elevator to chug its way up one story.

"Good to see you, Nicole," her advisor said as Nikki rushed in and dropped her handbag on the floor.

The woman must have gotten a job through some family connection. Whenever Nikki had a discussion with her, she seemed to know little about education.

"Sorry I'm late, Miss Bailey."

"Would you be Nicole if you weren't?"

Nikki ignored the sarcasm, although her ears burned and she wanted to retort something snarky. "My car wouldn't start and I had to find someone to help me."

"I'm not going to take up much of your time, Nicole, I'll just give you your good news and you can be on your way."

"Sure. You have my placement?"

"Yes, you will be doing your student teaching at Grayson High School."

"Where's that?"

"Portsmith."

"Portsmith? But Portsmith's, like, forty-five minutes away from here."

Miss Bailey sat back in her leather chair. Her hair glistened from way too much product and the sheen of her skin screamed for some powdering. "Nicole, if you wanted an assignment in Arcadia, you could have gotten your application in much earlier."

Nikki nodded. "First come, first served."

"Something like that." Miss Bailey picked up a piece of paper. "Let's see. Portsmith requires fingerprinting and a background check. They don't charge for it, unlike a lot of other school districts, so that'll save you a little money."

Nikki wanted to roll her eyes. She'd be spending a fortune on gas.

"You've been placed in a senior English class."

"I'm going to be teaching twelfth grade?"

"Your degree is in secondary English. What did you expect?"

"To start with sixth grade and work my way up."

Miss Bailey let out a forced laugh. "Doesn't work that way, Nicole. You take what you can get."

"Yes, ma'am."

"You'll meet your cooperating teacher the first day of your assignment, which is a week from tomorrow." Bailey handed her a folder. "Here's your letter of introduction and some forms you have to fill out and turn into Portsmith *before* your first day in the classroom."

"In other words, right away."

"You got it, Nicole. Don't mess up. Most of the student teacher slots are taken."

"Thank you," Nikki said and breezed out of Bailey's office. This was her last semester at Arcadia and she was glad to be through with it. Student teaching was something she'd looked forward to and couldn't wait to start.

After all of her delaying, she'd better take care of this now and get it over with. She wanted to be ready to roll on her first day. Although she hadn't spent a lot of time on this floor, she knew there was a break room somewhere. The corridor wrapped around the building in an L shape, and she eventually found it.

Seated in the student lounge, Nikki got busy on her paperwork. Fingerprints and background checks took time to process, so she needed to drop it off first thing in the morning.

A few students were scattered about the lounge, several with headphones or earbuds. Nikki never understood how people could get any work done with music piping into their ears.

A young woman stood by a vending machine counting her change, clearly frustrated. "Does anyone have a spare quarter?"

"Sure," Nikki said as she got up to hand it to her.

"Thank you." The young woman smiled.

As Nikki returned to her seat, she noticed no one else had budged. She returned to her paperwork and tried to get through it as thoroughly as possible.

"You made it."

Nikki looked up. There he was, the tall stranger who'd saved her from her car malfunction earlier, grinning and showing off his grill. That handsome smile could charm anyone.

Maybe even me.

"You're an education major?" Her heart palpitated, and she was amazed this young man had that effect on her.

"No, just here to take a business course."

"This is the education building." Why did he have to be so gorgeous?

"Yeah, well, the business program is overflowing and needed the space." He flashed his winning smile.

"Oh," Nikki said, her face a bit flushed. "Guess that means there's more job opportunities for you and less for me."

"Or the college just needs more space."

"Uh, yeah," Nikki murmured. She absently reached for her handbag and pulled out a tissue. She wanted to blot her forehead but didn't dare do it in front of him.

He's better than gorgeous. He's mesmerizing.

"You should have your connectors checked out as soon as you can."

"So you said outside." Nikki paused. "And thank you, again."

"Hey, no worries." He slung his backpack from one shoulder to the other. "So what you studying?"

"Education."

"Got that. What part?"

"English."

"Cool. I'll let you get back to work. Gotta run to class."

Nikki nodded. She was accustomed to seeing the same faces in her classes day after day. Apparently, it was possible to meet a whole new crowd by hanging out here after hours.

Business major.

He hardly looked the part. Perhaps he wanted to run a retail empire. Nikki glanced at her paperwork.

Why am I thinking about him?

Nikki pulled her driver's license out of her bag, eager to finish one form and move on to the next.

I don't even know his name.

**

Introduction to Marketing had seemed like a good idea at the time. Isaach could get his feet wet on a college campus to see if he liked it or not. He loved the vibe and the atmosphere on campus, but he couldn't concentrate today. Gettin' that crazy white girl off his mind proved to be impossible.

Dayum, she's fine.

Beautiful red hair, smokin' bod, and an attitude to match. A lady of few words, but that was all good. He had a hunch he'd be bumpin' into her again. The class had just started and had a long way to go.

His phone vibrated, and Isaach glanced at the message. *What time u done?* She asked the same question every time he went someplace, and he gave her the same answer. *When it's done.*

He put his phone down. Siera had become annoying. Datin' her didn't seem fun anymore. She was always getting all up in his business whether it concerned her or not. He was a man with a mission and goals, and answerin' to her at all hours was not on the agenda.

His phone vibrated again, and he ignored it. He'd paid for this class and he planned on getting his money's worth. Professor Drysdale's lecture was important, and Isaach needed to focus.

Shit, I didn't get her name.

She was an education major and that was all the information he had. Oh, and she drove an old, beat-up car. At least now he knew where to hang out if he wanted to run into her again. And he wouldn't mind getting another look at that pretty redhead.

A mousey-haired student sitting in front of him turned and gave him a furtive glance. A glance that was intrusive. Class had only been in session for a couple of weeks, but she'd done that last week as well. He wasn't interested and did his best to ignore her, but her expression twisted when she didn't get a reaction.

"Can I use that pen?" she said in a lethargic voice.

"Sure," Isaach whispered without making eye contact.

She snatched the extra pen from his desk and turned around.

He was accustomed to women looking at him. At six foot four, height alone made him stand out. But he didn't have time for the bullshit.

After class, Isaach hopped into his BMW and began the long drive back home. He cranked up the Reggie Snow and made his way toward Interstate 20. His mind drifted to that sexy young lady with the red hair and the car trouble.

Dayum, why didn't she tell me her name?

After she'd ignored his question outside, he had let it go when he'd bumped into her again in the lounge. But hey— he hadn't introduced himself either.

My bad.

That wouldn't happen again.

The florid mane. Emerald-green eyes that appeared luminescent in sunlight. Freckles that dotted her otherwise flawless complexion.

Oh, yeah. He'd make sure he would bump into the young lady again. And soon.

When he arrived at Siera's place, she already had the DVD on pause, the popcorn popped, and the soda on ice. Man, she was all set up and ready for him. Isaach shifted uncomfortably on the couch. This was too much for him. Too planned.

She lived in the basement of her parents' house with her own little setup. For her, that was a step toward independence.

Siera sat perched under his arm. From the soapy scent, he suspected she'd taken a bath and gotten all dolled up just to hangout at home. Her hair, all bunched up on top of her head, had that chemical smell of relaxer. A silly romantic comedy played on the television. She squealed at every sequence, but the movie—and ambiance—did nothing for him.

He preferred to be active. Go out, shoot hoops, chill with friends, convo, catch a real movie. Enjoy life. Siera didn't want to hang out with anyone else, and that didn't mesh with his lifestyle. He was nineteen and craved excitement. Siera was eighteen and craved boredom.

"Where's the remote?" she asked as the credits started to roll. Thankfully, they were at her place. Isaach didn't want to do this at his place. He'd made that mistake once and gotten his room torn up.

"Siera…"

"Oh, you wanna pick what we watch next?"

"No. I want to talk."

She looked at him, easing off his shoulder at the same time.

"What?"

"This isn't me."

"What?" she said again.

"Sitting around the crib, watching TV, doin' a whole lotta nothing."

"So what you wanna do?"

"I need to be out, around other people."

"So they can look at you, or you can look at them?"

Isaach could feel it coming. "That's not what it's all about, Siera. I'm just sayin' sitting on this couch is not for me."

"So you're sayin' you wanna go lie down?" She spoke without a hint of playfulness. Instead, she sounded sarcastic.

"No, what I'm sayin' is I don't want to be here."

Her expression turned even colder. "Who you fuckin'?"

Isaach let out an exasperated breath. She always went there. "It's not that."

"Who you fuckin'?"

He'd heard this before, and she never seemed to get it. Not wanting to be with her did not mean he wanted to be with someone else. "It's not about sex."

"I think it is with you. Everyone knows your rep."

"What's that supposed to mean?"

She pushed even farther away from him. "You and sex and the way you spreadin' it all over town."

Isaach stood up. "I'm not seeing or having sex with anyone else. If I were, it would still be irrelevant. The point is, I'm not the stay-at-home type. I need to be out doing things. I'm sorry, Siera, but this doesn't work for me. I'm outta here."

"Who you fuckin'? Sheila? Stacey? Joanne? LaShonda? Mavis? Who is it?"

Isaach made it to the door. "Good-bye, Siera."

She rose from her seat, fists clenched. "LaSonya? Charlotte? Joy?"

Isaach closed the door. She opened it right behind him and continued to call out names. He needed to get out. It was early—there had to be something going on at DaShon's crib.

He hated doing that. There was nothing worse than

breaking up with a girl, but it would be unfair to Siera to pretend to enjoy her lifestyle. She was a homebody and he was not. He needed to be around his friends. Siera wanted to only be around her man and no one else.

Isaach cruised his BMW down the driveway. She was a nice girl. He felt so damned guilty breaking up. Except it wasn't going to work.

That's life.

Isaach wanted a pizza. He'd pick one up before stopping by DaShon's. There was an assignment for his class that he should be working on, but it could wait. He needed to have some fun tonight to shake his mood and alleviate some of the guilt he felt over breaking up.

Isaach reached for his phone. He had House of Pizza on speed dial. "Yes, a large pepperoni for pickup."

CHAPTER TWO

Nikki had to download the Senior Applications in English curriculum and get familiar with it. She would have a week or two observing her cooperating teacher, then be expected to prepare lessons and teach.

Twelfth grade.

She had dropped off all her paperwork and gotten fingerprinted, so she should be good to go. She was anxious to meet her cooperating teacher. How was that going to work?

Nikki glanced around her dorm room. This would be her last year here. In a matter of months, she'd have to face the reality of finding an apartment.

What can I afford waiting tables?

She was determined to be self-sustaining. Hopefully, by the end of the semester, she'd land a full-time teaching position and make a real salary. Student teaching didn't pay, so she'd be teaching by day, waiting tables by night.

I'll go old and gray before I turn twenty-two.

Her dorm room wasn't really so bad. It had an eastern

exposure, so the room flooded with sunlight each morning. Her roommate, Carla, was never there because of her controlling, possessive boyfriend, who insisted she spend nights in his room. Nikki only imagined what his poor roommate had to go through, listening to their noisy lovemaking all night. Nikki had experienced those groans and moans on the one day that Carla and her boyfriend decided to do a quickie in her room because they couldn't wait to get back to his.

Like bunnies.

Nikki found the document online, Senior Applications in English, and downloaded it. Unit one was titled "Practicing Good Habits," with a suggested time frame of four weeks.

Huh? What does that have to do with English?

Maybe Nikki's old high school was different, but they'd done normal things like read literature. The curriculum had changed in four years, and Nikki was prepared to adapt. She wanted to make this career happen and was prepared to do whatever it took.

"What's up?" Carla said as she breezed through the door, her bob haircut bouncing along with her.

"What are you doing here?"

"Lunch," Carla said. "I still eat, ya know." She ran a hand through her thick dark hair.

"I wasn't aware Lover Boy let you eat."

Carla sighed. "Wanna join me?"

"Sure. I totally forgot about food today."

They stepped out of the dorm room and into the

beautiful north Louisiana afternoon. The cicadas were drumming full blast, and the scent of honeysuckle filled the air.

"I love the heat," Nikki mused.

"I hate it," Carla grumbled.

"But it's not humid."

"Whatever. So you ready to start your gig?"

"No. I have no clue what I'm going to do."

"But you've been looking forward to this."

"I know, but I don't know what I'm getting into yet. Have to see how it goes the first day."

"Bummer you have to drive so far."

Nikki shrugged. No use dwelling on that now. What she really needed was a grilled chicken sandwich on a sesame bun like they had at the Campus Grill.

The moment they walked in, Nikki caught a whiff of the grilled chicken and onions. A few people were scattered in seats around the perimeter of the place, by the windows, but it otherwise wasn't crowded. The buzz level was relatively low.

"How are you gonna do it?" Carla stared at the menu, cocking her head from one side to the other.

"Do what?"

"Pay for the gas. Teach all day, wait tables all night until you can't stand up anymore."

Carla had come from a good family. Her parents gave her whatever she needed. It was a testament to her character that she could sympathize with Nikki's struggles.

"Why don't you let me worry about that?" Nikki turned

to the bored cashier. "Grilled chicken. No fries."

"Tuna salad," Carla chirped. "With fries." Odd choice for a nutrition major.

"I'll get a table," Nikki said.

Carla had a point. It was going to be a struggle. Now, Nikki sat in a class all day before waiting tables. It would be another challenge altogether to drive forty-five miles, teach all day, then drive another forty-five miles to wait tables.

But how else can I be independent?

"Are you working today?" Carla placed her lunch on the table.

Nikki nodded. "Heading there after lunch."

"I think your chicken's ready."

Nikki glanced over at the counter. "It's so important."

"What? The chicken?"

"No, that I finish this program. I have to do whatever it takes."

**

The next morning, Nikki's alarm went off and she sat up in bed. She had a nagging feeling she'd forgotten something.

Gas.

She'd been so tired when she got off work last night that she'd forgotten to fill up the tank. That would be one more thing on her list to do before hitting the interstate.

After a quick shower, she selected a white dress that she felt was conservative enough for a teacher yet attractive enough for a twenty-one-year-old college student. She was straddling two worlds now and she had to maintain some kind of balance. Plus, she liked wearing white. It made her red hair stand out.

She ran her fingers over the fabric of the dress and gazed into her closet. Would she have enough clothes? She wasn't the world's best dresser in terms of variety. She'd be working five days a week as a student teacher and couldn't wear the same old things week after week.

Maybe a few good tip nights and I can splurge.

She had a good figure and wasn't shy about showing it off as long as she appeared tasteful. Might as well have a few more nice outfits. Or at least some more stuff to mix and match. Her phone chirped and she received a *good luck* text from Carla.

What's she doing up so early?

At least hair and makeup wouldn't be a long morning ordeal. She wore little on her face except for foundation and a light shade of lipstick. Her hair, after a good washing and blowout, was easy to manage.

Yogurt in hand, Nikki hurried out of the dorm and into her Camry. She needed to stop for gas and coffee, in that order. She liked to drink coffee in her room, but today, it was going to have to be on the go.

Grayson High School was easy enough to find. Nikki's GPS was correct for a change and she got there in about forty minutes. It was fairly close to the interstate, so she gauged her commute would not be as bad as she'd anticipated.

The building was a nondescript yet well maintained two-story brick structure. The grass seemed to be freshly cut and the structure had a recent paint job. Nikki found a spot in the visitors parking and crunched her feet across the gravel until she reached the entrance.

"Good morning. May I help you?"

"Good morning, I'm Nikki Dayton. I'm here to student teach."

"Yes, Mrs. Ramos is expecting you. Please have a seat."

Nikki sat on a wooden bench that thankfully had a cushion. She glanced around at the office, which was packed with mementoes, trophies, pictures, plaques, and other assorted junk. One plaque indicated the school had opened in 1969 as Centerdale High School and changed its name in 1981.

This place is ancient.

Another plaque attached to a portrait indicated the school was currently named after its first principal, Hortense Grayson. A woman with glasses and a prominent widow's peak graced the portrait.

"Miss Dayton."

Nikki looked up and saw a woman smiling. "Yes."

"I'm Claudia Ramos. Welcome to Grayson High."

"Thank you."

"I know you're anxious to see your classroom, but we need to take your picture to make you an ID badge. Come with me, please."

Mrs. Ramos led her down a short hallway.

"You have quite a commute, don't you?"

How about you don't remind me?

"Um, yes," Nikki said.

"We'll make your ID, then I'll walk you to your classroom."

Mrs. Ramos gestured into a room where a young man was seated behind a desk. Nikki dutifully posed for her picture and was sent back to Mrs. Ramos.

"That looks nice." Mrs. Ramos smiled.

It took a second for Nikki to register that Mrs. Ramos was looking at her ID.

"Come with me." Mrs. Ramos opened the office door. "Did you have a chance to look at our website?"

"Yes, I downloaded the school calendar and the bell schedule."

"Good. You'll need to refer to the bell schedule for a while until you memorize it. Oh, here's the cafeteria on the left. The lunches aren't bad here."

I'll believe that when I eat one.

"That's nice to know. I didn't think to bring anything for lunch."

They climbed the stairs to the second floor. B WING was painted in big letters on the stairwell wall. The interior had that sterile, industrial look of most mid-century schools.

Ramos paused before a door and knocked, then immediately pulled out a passkey and opened the door.

"Good morning," Ramos said, sounding a bit forced.

"Good morning."

"Sarah, this is Nicole Dayton. She's your student teacher. Take good care of her. Nicole, meet Sarah Paulson."

"Hi." Nikki extended her hand.

"Welcome," Sarah said, her voice emotionless.

Miss Paulson was about thirty. Her long black hair was pulled back in what appeared to be a very tight ponytail.

21

Had she volunteered to have a student teacher or had it been forced upon her?

"I'll leave you two to get acquainted. Nicole, I'm sure Sarah can answer any of your questions. If she can't, don't be shy. Come to me." Mrs. Ramos grinned and left the room.

Nikki glanced around the room. There were quite a few chairs, so she assumed Paulson must have some large classes. The windows looked out onto an athletic field. The bulletin boards were sparse.

"How long have you been teaching?" Nikki asked.

"This will be my eighth year."

Nikki nodded. "What's the daily schedule like?"

"As for now, here's a copy." Sarah handed her a piece of paper. "I've been in this business long enough to know they can change things around at the last minute."

Nikki looked over the schedule. Two periods of senior English, one senior English inclusion, and one of senior English advanced. "What's inclusion?"

"That's the class with all the special ed kids. You'll get another teacher for that period."

"For what?"

"You have to have a special ed teacher in the room. You can co-teach or work in small groups. You two can work that out."

"Why is third period blank?"

"Oh, that's your planning period. You'll be doing most of your work then, such as lesson planning, calling parents, making copies, whatever."

Nikki began to realize this assignment was going to be a ton of work. Then again, college was a ton of work. She could handle it.

"For the first week or two, you can just watch me," Sarah said. "You can take notes, ask questions, and get to know the kids."

"That sounds good."

"By the third week, you take over teaching the classes. I'll be around for support, but you're in charge."

Nikki smiled, but it was a nervous smile. This was going to take some getting used to. At least she had two weeks to get ready.

"Do you have an extra notebook?" Nikki silently cursed herself for not being prepared.

"Sure," Sarah said. "The supply closet's over there. Grab what you need."

Nikki found a spiral notebook and a pen.

"By the end of the week, I'll have a folder for you with seating charts and all that. I'm sure I'll be moving 'em around a lot at first."

Sarah seemed comfortable with her job. Nikki's palms sweated. She was nervous as hell but tried not to show it.

"Where do you want me to sit?"

Paulson pointed to a chair. "For the first day, you can sit and observe. The rest of the week it might be a good idea for you to be on your feet moving around the room. You want 'em to get used to your presence."

Nikki nodded. "Got it."

A shrill clanging burst through the room.

"There's the bell," Sarah said.

Children soon began filing in. Except they weren't really children. They were seniors. Young adults, and many of them taller than Nikki, passed by her to take a seat.

"'Sup."

Nikki was greeted that way by many walking into the room. They probably assumed she was another student. Sarah immediately began teaching. She didn't do any of the first-day getting-to-know-you activities that Nikki had practiced in her college classes.

They're seniors. I guess they know the drill.

After Sarah finished her mini-lesson, she took attendance. Nikki made a note to do that first. She intended to learn from Sarah, not copy her.

"I hear she's tough," a student whispered.

Nikki shrugged.

Yeah, they think I'm a student.

Sarah hadn't introduced her. Could that be an oversight?

"She's putting me to sleep," another student whispered.

Nikki smiled and made a note in her spiral not to be boring. The morning crawled along, but she somehow made it through two periods of senior English. She had the luxury of lunch and her planning period back to back, and she took advantage of that time to explore the high school.

The students wore different-colored ID badges than the staff, so Nikki got some odd looks from staff members who had no clue who she was.

"Where's the staff restroom?" Nikki thought it was a perfectly innocent question to ask a staff member she passed in the hallway.

The woman looked down at her ID, then back up to Nikki. "Across from the library. Down this hallway and to your left."

Nikki thought saying thanks would be disingenuous, since all she got was attitude, so she smiled and nodded.

Fourth period was her favorite class of the day so far. The inclusion students were a livelier group. She had a feeling she would enjoy working with them. Fourth period breezed by, then the last class of the day arrived.

"Well, look who's here."

Nikki turned. It was the same towering black man who had helped her with her car at Arcadia College.

CHAPTER THREE

He looked every bit as gorgeous as she'd remembered. The hair cut close to his scalp. The long arms protruding from his sleeveless jersey. The perfectly coordinated shorts and shoes. And that killer smile.

Her ears burned and chest tightened. Crickets hopped in her tummy, and her palms moistened.

"Hello," Nikki said. Her voice came out barely a croak. How in the world did he end up here?

"What brings you to Grayson?" he asked, his voice smooth.

"I'm a student teacher here."

"Great. I'm a student."

He's got to be kidding.

"I thought you were a student at Arcadia?"

"Naw, just taking one class there. I'm a senior here."

"And you make that drive all the way for one class?"

"And you make this drive every day for a job that doesn't pay?"

Unfortunately, they had attracted the attention of Miss Paulson.

"Is something wrong?" she asked.

He shook his head and so did Nikki. The young man took a seat a few rows away. His long ebony legs stretched out from the desk, which seemed too small for such a tall man.

"Do you have any questions?" Sarah asked Nikki.

"No, not yet. Thanks."

When roll call was taken, Nikki finally learned the young man's name.

Isaach Madison.

He was on the basketball team. No surprise there. He was tall, had a gorgeous smile and a lean muscular build. It was difficult not to ogle him.

This period was the advanced class, so it was safe to assume he was smart. He had one foot in the door at a college, so he clearly had goals. And if his attire was any indication—today he wore red—he had no shortage of money to spend on clothing.

He glanced at her and smiled. A warm smile. Inviting.

Why am I thinking about him?

This had been a long day. First days on any job were always tough. Tomorrow would be better. Plus, she still had to put in a shift at the restaurant tonight.

"Sorry, didn't mean to be a smartass before."

Nikki looked up from her notes. Isaach towered over her. He had the most beautiful complexion she'd seen on a man. Perfectly clear. Not a blemish in sight.

"Maybe," she said.

He extended his hand. "Isaach Madison."

She glanced down at his big hand. She placed her tiny one in his, and he devoured it with his palm. "Nikki Dayton."

Heat surged through her core at his touch. If a handshake could do that, what else was Mr. Madison capable of? He was a student. Technically, *her* student. She had to check herself.

"I guess I have to call you Miss Dayton." The playfulness in his voice wasn't lost on her.

"I guess that would be right." Remaining professional with Isaach was already a challenge. If he bottled his charm, he'd be rich.

"How's the car doin'?"

"Fine."

"Hey, are you really gonna drive all the way back to Arcadia?"

"I have to," Nikki said. "I need to work tonight." She paused for a second. "At my *paying* job."

"Okay, fair enough. See you tomorrow." Isaach flashed her another smile before heading out the door.

Miss Paulson slunk up behind her. "Is there a problem, Nikki?"

"No, not at all."

"I thought he was bothering you."

"No, he's just someone who helped me with my car."

"Isaach? Get his hands dirty? Not a chance. His family does everything for him."

"Oh, I do have a question. Do you want me to call you Sarah or Miss Paulson?"

"It's Miss Paulson to you."

Well, I asked.

The learning curve on this job was steep. Nikki grabbed her stuff, said good night to Sarah—um, Miss Paulson—and was on her way.

**

Nikki reported to her job, about two miles from campus. It was a family restaurant, more of a diner, and did good business. The tips had made a big difference in her life. Paid for textbooks. Gas. Food.

"You ready for tomorrow?"

Nikki glanced over at Don. She was busy clearing a table and didn't really have time to chat. "No."

Don was an oily-nosed frat boy who unfortunately had a job at the same restaurant as Nikki. He was a little on the chubby side and had red hair that badly needed a comb.

"Must be a lot of work. I mean, to be a student teacher."

"No," Nikki lied and placed the dishes on the bus cart.

"You want to do something after work?"

Nikki wanted to laugh at him, except it really wasn't funny. "No. Any more questions?"

Don shook his head. "Just askin'."

Nikki pushed the bus cart to her next table. Don was a pain in the ass. He always made some lame attempt to ask her out without saying anything specific. Not that she was even remotely interested in him.

She got the impression he asked her out due to proximity rather than interest, since they happened to work at the same place. Had he noticed her on campus, he probably wouldn't have the nerve to say anything.

And what the hell was he doing here anyway? His shift should have ended by now.

Nikki wasn't having a good night. First, jitters from the first day on a new job, and now she dealt with a heavy shift at work.

"How can you be out of corn? Doesn't it come in a can?"

"I'll double-check," Nikki said.

"Don't bother. Just bring me the carrots."

Nikki smiled at the irate customer and moved on to the next table. "How's everything?"

The woman looked up and gave Nikki a sour look. "Glad you asked. I said a spinach omelet, not Spanish. I don't like spicy food."

"I'm sorry, I'll take care of that right away."

She disappeared into the kitchen and put the offending omelet down.

"Carl, spinach omelet. That's spinach, not Spanish, I'm sorry!"

"No problem."

She leaned against the counter for a moment and glanced at the clock. Her shift would end in less than thirty minutes. Hopefully, she'd sleep well tonight.

When she finally punched out, she exhaled. A long, trying day. Now she just had to make it to her dorm room and pass out.

The night air was still warm as she went out the back door.

"Hey, Nikki."

The voice startled her. It was Don, leaning up against the side of the building. She was a few feet away from him but could smell the liquor on his breath.

"You wanna do something?"

"No."

"Well I need a designated driver. I can't drive like this."

"I'm not your designated anything. Call one of your frat boys."

"Come on, Nikki, help me out." He moved toward her. At times, her heart went out to him. Even though he was a frat boy in a fairly popular frat on campus, he was still a loner. He had no clue how to express himself.

"I'm not giving you a ride, Don." When had he had time to get so drunk? He had seemed fine half an hour ago. He must have had a bottle in his car and chugged it down to get up the nerve to ask her out.

"Please." Don grabbed her arm tightly.

"Let go!" she said.

"Please, Nikki. Let's do something." He squeezed her arm harder.

Her knee went flying up and made contact with Don's groin. He collapsed to the ground, with a thud and more than a few howls. She hadn't wanted to hurt him, but damn, he was being a beast and far too aggressive.

Nikki got into her car and drove away. Although shaken, she was still concerned for his safety in the state he was in. She'd let someone at the frat know where he was when she got back on campus.

This is not a good way to end the day.

**

Isaach cruised along in his car with a stiff cock between his legs. He'd hoped Nikki hadn't noticed the tent when he was speaking with her in class earlier.

Dayum, she's hot.

He loved her red hair and classy style of dress. He sat behind the wheel, turned on Rockie Fresh, and tried not to think of the hot student teacher, but it wasn't easy.

This is gonna be one hell of a year.

How could he concentrate on fifth period English with Nikki's curvy body distracting him? She had a nice shape, which was obvious the first day he'd met her. She also had something else, a quality he couldn't really put his finger on yet. He needed to find out what it was that attracted him to her.

"'Sup," Isaach said after grabbing his phone. It was DaShon. "Good day. First day of my last year of high school, that's wassup." Isaach lowered the phone for a second as he caught a glimpse of a police car passing. "Sorry, yeah. Sounds good."

He didn't want to a get a ticket for using his cell phone in a school zone, which was exactly what he was doing.

"Wanna join me at the club?"

DaShon meant at the billiards club, and he was at a table right in front when Isaach entered.

"Sup." DaShon had one of those long, angular faces. He was tall, although not quite as tall as Isaach. He kept his hair buzzed almost to his scalp, and had zigzag designs through it. Considering how short he kept his hair that design would grow out in no time. Which was what DaShon wanted. Then he could get a new one.

"Sup."

"How was the first day of school for you?"

Isaach looked at the ceiling, then back at DaShon. "Ah, don't remind me."

"One mo' year; it'll race by."

"I hope so," Isaach said, suddenly not so sure he wanted it to. "How was yours?"

"Junior year? Nothing special." DaShon paused. "Siera came around here earlier."

Isaach frowned. "She's gotta let go."

DaShon went back to the pool table. That was one thing Isaach loved about DaShon. He could read Isaach and understand when he didn't want to talk about something. DaShon was seventeen and had street smarts that Isaach could only dream about.

As much as he tried to put her out of his mind, his thoughts kept drifting back to Nikki. He was drawn to her. That was how his days at school were going to go now— he'd spend all day looking forward to fifth period.

"You wanna shoot some?"

Isaach nodded and picked up a pool stick. What he really wanted to do was ask out Nikki, but he wasn't sure how that would work out. Technically, she would be his fifth period teacher, even though she was student teaching. Plus she had a job after school.

Then it came to him. He'd need to catch up with her on

the Arcadia College campus, away from the nosy eyes of Miss Paulson. Maybe on a night off, if she had one.

I wonder where Nikki works?

The next morning, Isaach jiggled his foot as he sat in class. It was only second period and he longed for his fifth period class so he could see Nikki.

Can't call her that.

He'd have to address her as Miss Dayton at Grayson, so he'd better get used to it. Between Grayson High School and Arcadia College, they'd have a lot in common. Perhaps too much.

His phone made that telltale sign he had a text, so he snuck a peek at it. *What lunch you got?*

He sent a text back to DaShon. *First.*

Isaach tried to focus his attention on calculus, but it just wasn't happening. He kept thinking about the beautiful red-haired woman he wanted so badly to get to know. Where did she live? What did she do with her free time? What kind of fragrances did she wear?

When lunchtime came, he headed to the cafeteria.

"Hey, Isaach, over here." He joined DaShon at the lunch table. Isaach's gaze prowled around the cafeteria, searching for signs of a certain redhead.

Oh, shit, she'd be eating in the teacher's lounge.

That was another thing he needed to keep straight in his head. She was a student at Arcadia, just like him, but a teacher here. He was still a student.

"What is this anyway?" DaShon asked.

"Turkey Tetrazzini."

"Turkey Tetra-huh?" DaShon looked puzzled.

"Just eat it; it's good. We had this last year, you don't remember?"

"Naw."

Isaach glanced left and right.

"What you keep lookin' around for?"

"Nothing," Isaach said.

"Nothing right. You lookin for somethin' or someone."

Isaach looked at him. DaShon dove his fork into his turkey Tetrazzini.

"Is it that obvious?" Isaach asked.

DaShon nodded.

Isaach ate his lunch, but it wasn't easy. He wanted to discover what it was about Nikki that he found so alluring.

"What you doin' after school?" DaShon asked.

"Not sure yet but hopefully having some fun."

Determined to enjoy his last year of high school, Isaach planned to make the most of his senior year. Go out. Meet new people. Explore new places.

He had long-term goals, including college, although he wasn't sure if Arcadia was going to be his first choice. He still had time to consider his options.

At nineteen, he should have been out of here by now, but he was paying the price for being so unfocused when he was much younger. He wanted to have some fun but at the same time stay focused on the future.

"What about that class you take?"

"That's only one day a week." Isaach glanced around the

room, hoping Siera didn't have first lunch. He hadn't seen her yesterday, so that was a good sign. It made him uncomfortable that she was sniffing around for him at the billiards hall.

"Hey, can you give me a ride after school?"

"Sure," Isaach said. "Where you need to go?"

"You know," DaShon said.

"Oh, yeah, you chillin' at her place today. Gotcha."

"Thanks, bro."

Isaach didn't mind helping out DaShon. He had been a good friend, even though he had a lot on his plate. Isaach encouraged DaShon to stay in school. He faced a lot of family pressure to drop out and get a job.

Fortunately, Isaach had no such pressure from his family. They were all for his education and taking it as far as he wanted to go. He was lucky.

After what seemed liked forever, fifth period finally arrived. Isaach eagerly made his way to senior English advanced. When he entered the room, he greeted Nikki with a broad smile. She pressed her lips together and looked away. Miss Paulson was hovering over her, and Isaach remembered this was not the place. He needed to get to know her elsewhere.

I'll make it happen.

CHAPTER FOUR

A rush of warmth permeated Nikki's face when Isaach had smiled at her.

He'd become more appealing by the day. First of all, he personified tall, dark, and gorgeous. Also well dressed, well mannered, and well groomed, he had an undeniable presence. During fifth period, it had become difficult for Nikki to focus on anything else but him.

Recalling what Miss Paulson had said, Nikki remained on her feet, monitoring the classroom. She found this to be most helpful during fourth period, as the special needs students were full of questions. But this wasn't fourth period. This was fifth period, the class with the elephant in the room.

"Are you going to be our teacher for the rest of the year?" a student sitting on the aisle asked.

"No, just the first semester."

Nikki continued around the room, careful to avoid the corner where Isaach sat.

"Can you help me with this?"

"Have you tried it on your own yet?" Nikki cocked her head to one side to look at the student's blank paper.

"No."

Nikki smiled. "Why don't you give it a try first?"

Miss Paulson gave Nikki a nod of approval. She continued to move around the room, which seemed like a pretty easy job. She felt sure she could handle this part. It was all the planning she wasn't so sure about.

Against her better judgment, she glanced over at Isaach and momentarily went light-headed from the sight of him. He appeared to be completely focused on what he was doing.

That's a good sign.

Miss Paulson had finally given in and given them one of those getting to know you assignments. Nikki was eager to read Isaach's, but she didn't dare.

I'll peek over his shoulder.

She slowly circled around the room until she came in close proximity to Isaach's desk. He was seated in the back of the room, so it was easy for her to slip behind him.

He wore his usual outfit of coordinated cap, sleeveless shirt, shorts, and athletic shoes. Today's color was blue. With his long arms, he must be a good athlete. She made a mental note to catch one of the games once basketball season started.

"Miss Dayton."

Nikki's attention shot over to Miss Paulson.

"There's an odd number in the class. Would you fill one out?"

"Sure." Nikki took a paper from her. The exercise

involved not putting a name on the paper. Just fill out the facts, shuffle the papers, and try to figure out what kind of person the answers represented.

She found an empty desk and dutifully completed the form. There were basic questions like favorite color, music type, and foods. The questions then became more interesting, asking about preferences for outdoors, evening activities, and dream vacations.

"When everyone's finished, please pass them up to the front," Miss Paulson instructed. The students who'd finished complied while others hurried to write something down.

"Can I have a volunteer to redistribute them?"

Isaach raised his hand.

"Thank you, Isaach." Miss Paulson continued, "If you get your own, please trade with someone else. Oh, and Isaach, please pick up the few remaining ones before you redistribute."

Isaach nodded and picked up the few who hadn't passed them forward, including Nikki's. He slipped hers to the bottom of the stack.

No, he's not going to…

Sure enough, Isaach walked over to his desk, placed hers down, and continued passing out the rest of the papers.

"Any volunteers to analyze first? Miss Dayton, why don't you call on someone?"

Nikki glanced down at her seating chart. "Shania?"

"Remember, Shania," Miss Paulson said, "I want you to infer. Use the information to draw inferences about this person."

"Um, she likes the outdoors, likes hot weather, and likes to dance."

"Good. How do you know it's a she?"

"The writing is girly."

"Okay." Miss Paulson frowned. "Not sure about that one, but we'll go with it. Next?"

Paulson called on a quiet young man in the front row. "Justin?"

"Um, this person likes to swim, probably is into music, and has possibly never left Portsmith."

"Hmm, interesting. Why do you say that?"

"Their idea of a dream vacation is going to the water park."

That elicited more than a fair share of laughs from the classroom.

"Okay, whoever you are, we are not laughing at you but laughing with you. Miss Dayton?"

"Pick someone?"

"No, your turn."

"Oh." Nikki looked at her paper. "Let's see. This person enjoys camping so I'm going to infer they really love the outdoors. They like to look at the stars at night, so I'm going to infer astronomy is a favorite part of science class. Their idea of a dream vacation is to get out of the United States, so I'll infer they might be yearning for an adventure."

Paulson pressed her lips together in a forced smile. "That's nice. Any volunteers?"

Nikki hoped she didn't pick Isaach. Several more people read before, ultimately, Paulson called on him.

"This lovely lady likes to swim, so I'll infer she believes the ocean is vast and ready to explore."

Paulson interrupted. "I'm sorry, how do you know it's a she?"

"Her favorite color is pink." Isaach glanced at Nikki. She caught his glance and looked away.

"That doesn't mean anything these days." Paulson cleared her throat. "Continue."

"Her favorite nighttime activity is to light scented candles and take a hot bath, so I'll infer she wants a man to make love to her all night."

Paulson rolled her eyes. "Wrap it up, Isaach."

"Her idea of a dream vacation is exploring the Scottish Highlands, so I'll infer she's a woman after my own heart. I'd like to do the same thing."

"Very romantic, Isaach. Next?"

Nikki didn't have her handbag close by to do a quick check with her compact, but she was certain her face had turned pink.

**

Isaach meandered around the parking lot. He searched for Nikki's Camry but couldn't spot it. If he hung out by the exit door long enough, he'd catch her when she left. He didn't wait long. Within a short time, she headed out of the building at a brisk pace.

"Hey, miss, you in a hurry?" Like that wasn't obvious.

Her hair swept across her face from the breeze. Sunglasses concealed her eyes, but her pouty red lips made him want to take her in his arms and kiss her. But not in the parking lot.

"Gotta go to work."

"You okay?"

She paused, tilted her head, and inhaled. "Yeah, why?"

"Your face looks kinda pink. I hope I didn't embarrass you in class today."

"Of course not. How could you have?" She exhaled, then took another deep breath and her breasts thrust forward.

"My interpretation of your answers."

"No one knew it was me. Including you."

She continued walking, and Isaach kept up with her.

"How's the car?"

"Very good, thank you. How's yours?"

"Oh, it's great. Listen, I know it's kind of awkward talking around here. Can we catch up at Arcadia sometime?"

Nikki looked at him. Or at least looked in his direction. He couldn't tell through her shades. "Perhaps."

"Perhaps?"

"Yeah, perhaps. I like that word a lot better than maybe. Don't you?"

Isaach smiled. "I never thought of that."

"Look, I gotta get to work."

"So you said. Do you work on Monday?"

"Don't have my schedule yet for next week." She flung her door open, threw her bags in the back seat, and got inside.

"Okay, I have my class on Monday. Maybe we can meet up after."

Nikki's face relaxed for a moment. She even smiled.

"We'll see. Okay, Isaach?" She closed her car door.

"Okay. Later, Miss D."

She backed her Camry out of her parking space and headed out of the lot. He strolled back to his BMW, somewhat satisfied with himself. Arcadia College. That would work. He was determined to see her on more neutral ground.

He got a text. *Where are you?*

He'd promised DaShon a ride and had forgotten. *Meet me at the front door.*

Isaach appreciated the company, because otherwise he'd just be thinking about Nikki. He could be wrong about her. He knew nothing about her, really. Until they had time to sit down and talk, do something, get to know one another, he was just speculating.

DaShon's lady didn't live far from the school. This part of the Portsmith Independent School District, called Centerdale, was an old part of town with a diverse socio-economic background. There were families with plenty of money and others with none, all living within blocks of one another.

Isaach received another text. *Hey wanna watch a movie?* He showed the phone to DaShon. "Can you believe this?"

DaShon squinted his eyes to read the text. "Siera doesn't get it."

"She just wants what a thirty-year-old wants."

DaShon laughed. "What does a thirty-year-old want?"

"Stay home all the time, I guess." Isaach wasn't sure if he wanted to know the answer, but he asked DaShon anyway.

"You ever have sex with a teacher?"

"Yeah, old lady Hallet."

"WTF?"

"It was her last year and she was retiring so I don't think she really cared what she did."

"But she was like a hundred years old."

"Close. She was fifty-four."

"So what happened?"

"I went to her after school for tutoring. I could tell she was hot for me. One day she *forgot* about our tutoring session and called me from home. Said I could stop by her place. I did and she gave me some head."

"Hallet? When?"

"Yup. Last year."

"Gave you head?"

"Yeah, damn good too. The lady had skills. Why, who you hot for?"

"No one."

"Then why'd you ask?"

"No reason."

"Yeah, right. You hot for someone."

Isaach wasn't thinking about sex, but rather the personal interaction between teacher and student. Approaching Nikki at Grayson was not a good idea. He had to keep it at the college, where they were both students.

But does that make it okay?

CHAPTER FIVE

It was only second period and Nikki had a headache. Miss Paulson was having a bad day and took it out on her. Paulson repeatedly asked her to pass out papers, collect papers, or run small errands.

She's treating me more like a teacher's aide than a student teacher.

She looked forward to third period so she could get a break. She was anxious for this observation period to be over with so she could start teaching.

Maybe then I can boss Paulson around.

Nikki saw enough of what to do and what not to do. Today was day three and she had a pretty good handle on how things worked. She made a mental note to start next week setting some expectations of her own. Expectation number one would be to tell Paulson to stop treating her like an aide.

"Miss, can you help me?" a student asked.

"Do you have a question?"

"What does it mean to analyze?"

"It means to think about what you've read, process it in your mind, and make sense of it." Nikki hoped her explanation made sense.

"I don't like to think." The boy grimaced.

"What have you been doing for the past eleven years?"

Now the boy looked completely bewildered. Nikki probably shouldn't have said that, but it was too late now.

"I don't know." The boy paused. "I guess I'll have to think about that one."

She gave him a high five and moved on.

"Miss—"

"Dayton."

"Miss Dayton, is it break time yet?"

"I'll let you know."

Nikki needed a break from Paulson's crabby mood. Her stomach grumbled and she glanced at the clock. Lunch was only minutes away. She craved food and some alone time.

Finally, she stood in line in the cafeteria. Once again, she'd forgotten to prepare a lunch. She had a choice between beef stroganoff and a baked potato with all the fixings. She went for the baked potato with sour cream, cheese, butter, chives, and broccoli. Four dollars later, she couldn't remember where the teachers' lounge was located.

A security guard stood nearby.

"Excuse me," Nikki said. "Can you point me in the direction of the teachers' lounge?"

"I'll do one better than that. Let me walk you there." The guard gestured with his arm. "Right this way."

"Thank you."

"Miss Dayton, correct?"

"Yes."

"You remember my name?" the guard asked.

Nikki flashed a smile. "I've met so many people in three days…"

"Mr. Da'Trin. How you like it here so far?"

"It's been keeping me busy."

"Good answer. It only gets busier."

Mr. Da'Trin opened the door for her, which was helpful as she gripped her lunch tray with both hands.

"Thank you, sir."

"Anytime, miss."

She sat down, grateful to relieve her exhausted feet. She needed to formulate a game plan to make this gig work. It was supposed to be all about her getting experience teaching, not experience being an aide. Then again, she couldn't really blame Miss Paulson. Nikki hadn't taken any initiative yet.

"How's it going?" a young lady asked.

"Fine, thank you. Anyone sitting here?"

"No, go right ahead. I'm Sheryl Moore."

"Nikki Dayton."

"You're a new teacher?"

"Student teacher."

"Oh, from where?"

"Arcadia College."

"And they sent you here? Isn't that kinda far?"

Nikki sighed. "Yeah, well, kinda got my paperwork in late."

"Ah. So who's your cooperating teacher?"

"Sarah Paulson."

Sheryl rolled her eyes. "Good luck."

"What do you mean?"

"Oh, nothing. She was my co-op teacher a few years ago. She'll disappear after a while."

"Disappear?"

"Take on another class. That way you'll have the students all to yourself."

"Oh, that's good. I guess." Nikki buttered her potato.

"It is. It's the only way you'll develop your own teaching style. She's not gonna be in the room with you once you start teaching. At least not for more than a few days."

"That's a relief. Any other tips?"

Sheryl paused for a moment. "Just make each class your own."

Nikki nodded. "So does she not like student teachers or something?"

"I would think on the contrary. She volunteers to be a co-op teacher. They can't make anyone do it."

"Wow. I didn't know that." Nikki scooped up a forkful of her lunch.

"Like a lot of teachers, she's set in her ways. I mean, she's not that old, but after a few years, you kinda get into a groove, I guess."

"Where did you go to college?"

"Monroe."

"Convenient."

"Yeah, it's close by. I don't know how you make that drive from Arcadia every day."

Let me hear that comment one more time.

"I suppose I'll get used to it."

Fourth period went fine because she liked the kids in that class. They engaged her. She engaged them and hoped she got through to them. That was what this gig was all about. Learning how to become a teacher by practical experience in a classroom.

Fifth period brought Isaach Madison. No matter how hard she tried to resist, Nikki's attention continued to drift toward him. He was like a magnet. In addition to being one of the best looking young men she'd ever seen, he gave her a compelling desire to be near him.

But why?

She hadn't figured that out.

"Good afternoon." Isaach greeted her with a warm smile.

"Good afternoon, Isaach." She gravitated toward his corner of the classroom. "How's your day going?"

"Doin' good, doin' good. Like a brutha should."

"How's your schedule?"

"Didn't I ask you that yesterday?"

"I mean your class schedule."

Isaach leaned back. "Let's see, I got boys' athletics, calculus, civics, environmental science, and your fine class."

Nikki's face flushed. She placed a palm against her cheek.

"Miss Dayton." Miss Paulson's voice could chill a cup of hot coffee.

Nikki glanced at her.

"Can you pass these out, please?"

Nikki turned to the class. "You heard Miss Paulson, let's

have a volunteer." She called on the first person that raised their hand, and then walked away to get Paulson out of her line of vision. She was sure the teacher was steaming, but she didn't care. It was time for Nikki to be assertive.

"Miss Dayton?"

Nikki turned to see a young woman. "Yes?"

"When does tutoring start?"

Although the question caught her off guard, she had a quick answer. "I haven't made the schedule yet."

Am I expected to tutor as well?

When would she squeeze it in? She couldn't really do much after school with her work schedule.

Paulson watched Nikki like a cat eyeing a bird.

I might have to ignore Isaach while she's in the room.

Although he was impossible to ignore. He was too attractive, and she was far too attracted to him. When class ended, Isaach lingered outside the door. With a quick glance at Paulson, Nikki slipped out and started walking.

"Look, I can't wait till Monday. Is it okay to see you this weekend?

"I'm working."

"I know, but I mean when you have some time."

"Usually pull a double on weekends. We'll see."

"Which dorm are you in?"

"Brittany." Nikki wasn't sure why she was giving him that information. It just sort of slipped out of her mouth. But—she wanted him to have it.

"Okay, see you."

She moved away from him before Paulson stuck her nose

out the door. After a quick trip to the ladies' room, she returned to the classroom. Teachers technically couldn't leave until twenty minutes after the students were dismissed.

"How's it going for you?" Paulson asked in a somewhat singsong voice.

"Terrific," Nikki said. "I'm ready to teach."

"Are you?"

She was in no mood for a confrontation but sensed one coming from Paulson. "That's what I'm here for."

"If you don't mind my asking, how old are you?"

"Twenty-one."

"You know there are students in this class only two and three years younger than you."

"And?"

Paulson hesitated, but her eyes still looked at Nikki with a hard glare. "All I'm saying is that they're your students, not your peers. Don't confuse them with your friends."

"Duly noted."

Oh, gimme a break.

Nikki left the classroom, questioning her judgment in giving Isaach her dorm name. It wasn't like he was going to stalk her. He lived here in Portsmith and was only in Arcadia for one class. But she needed to be prepared if he stopped by this weekend. By giving him the dorm, she'd essentially invited him over.

**

Saturday, Isaach needed to work on his assignment for his college class. That gave him another reason to drive to

Arcadia. He could use the library and hopefully meet with Nikki as well. Although his time would probably be wiser spent working on calculus for his high school class. He needed that credit.

He rolled the top down instead of blasting the AC. The day was beautiful and promised to get even better. His BMW cruised along the interstate and he was there before he knew it. The drive suddenly didn't feel so long after all.

As he strolled along the college campus headed for the library, he heard his name called.

"Hey, Isaach." It was Rhonda. She'd been a senior at Grayson last.

"Hey, what's up?"

"Just headin' to the mall. What's up with you?"

"I came here to use the library."

"Long drive for a library. You still at Grayson, aren't you?"

"You know it. My last year."

He'd hooked up with Rhonda a few times last year, but it was never anything serious.

"Good to see you, Isaach. Pop my number into your cell so you can come by my room later."

He felt that uncomfortable empty feeling in the pit of his stomach. "Naw, can't do that. Got work to do."

"Since when is work so important to you?" Her tone was less than pleasant.

"Nice to see you, Rhonda." He kept a brisk pace as he headed to the library. Two eyes probably glared at his back right now.

Dayum.

Isaach had loyalty to a woman he barely knew. He had some sort of connection with Nikki, and he needed to find out what it was and why. It wasn't his usual style at all. Then again, at nineteen, he wasn't so sure he really had a style.

He should at least leave a message for her. It took no time at all to find her on Facebook. He wondered how long it would take before the school district asked her to delete her profile. According to DaShon, that's what had happened with Mrs. Hallet.

He left a message on her page, but if she was at work, he doubted she'd get it. He strolled over to her dorm to leave a note.

He had to navigate his way around campus before finally finding the Brittany. He handwrote a note with his cell phone number and location and signed it "a fellow college student." Hopefully the security guard at the front desk would get the message to her.

Why didn't I just ask her where she works?

It was rude to visit people at work. That would have been a bad idea. He'd stick to the plan.

In the library, concentrating on a research paper just wasn't happening. The library closed early on the weekend, so he wasn't sure what he was going to accomplish. Isaach buried his face in his hands in an attempt to clear his mind.

He had goals. He planned on college next year—although he was not sure which one—to study business and play basketball. He could land some full scholarships, not for the money but for the prestige. He didn't need the cash to pay for college. His family took care of that. But he did need a high-profile recruitment if he chose to pursue basketball as a career. His family was supportive of his goals and highly prioritized education.

So why am I making Nikki Dayton a priority?

CHAPTER SIX

Nikki pulled her car into the lot outside her dorm and hauled her butt inside. It had been a long day, but not as bad as she'd expected.

"Hey, Nikki. You got a note," the young woman behind the desk said as she slung a handbag over her shoulder.

"Thanks. Have a good night." Nikki grabbed her mail and picked up the note before taking the elevator to her floor.

She threw her stuff down on the table and plopped on the couch. She was tired and grateful Carla was off with Mr. Wonderful. She needed some peace and quiet time.

After she clicked on the TV to find some mindless entertainment, she put her feet up on the ottoman and leaned back. This would be a great time to relax, but she couldn't. She was restless.

Curious about the note, she unfolded it. Isaach had written his phone number. Her heart palpitated, and her cheeks warmed. He was here. That put her in an awkward position, because now it was up to her to contact him or not.

He didn't have her number. It was her move or no move.

She tossed the paper down, not ready to make that decision.

I need a shower.

She had a lot to think about. Mrs. Ramos had called her and asked if Nikki could please have lesson plans ready for Monday. Apparently she was ready to reassign Miss Paulson to another class.

Thank God for small favors.

Nikki was prepared to take the reins of her own class. She wasn't learning anything from Paulson, who only served as a distraction. Nikki stepped into the hot shower and let the streaming jets of water do their job.

When she finished, she was hungry. She hadn't eaten anything at the restaurant because she couldn't stand eating their food every day. The note with Isaach's number beckoned to her.

It's up to me now.

She gazed at the piece of paper tossed onto the table in front of her, and then she glanced at her phone.

She shouldn't call. And she should most definitely not get involved with a student. She was his teacher for all intents and purposes. Isaach looked at it from that perspective, which was fine.

Is it fine?

No, it's not fine. It would be foolish—and playing with fire—to get involved with him.

Who's talking about getting involved?

All he said was that he was on campus and dropped his

digits. Nikki could call him and hang out with him in the library, because that would be innocent enough. Or just text him and say thanks for saying hi. Or get with him to get something to eat. That should be fine.

He's the one who's fine.

When he'd spoken to her at school, he made her feel like she was the only person in the room. He completely focused on her, and that made Nikki's cheeks burn.

Her heart pounded. As she got dressed, she carefully chose something appealing should she decide to respond to his note. A black dress that carefully accented her red hair. And a pair of killer shoes.

She took a deep breath. "Here it goes." She entered Isaach's digits into her phone and sent a text. *Still in the library?*

In a very short time, she got a response. *No, moved to The Grill.*

Nikki texted, *See u there.*

Heat surged through her. The anticipation of joining him made her light-headed, and her heartbeat increased. Even though she shouldn't. Even though it was so wrong. Even though it could come back to haunt her.

She checked herself in the mirror, dabbed on a touch of fragrance, and grabbed her handbag.

She carefully made her way across to the Campus Grill. How long had he been waiting? Her shoes clicked against the pavement, and her nerves rattled.

Isaach sat drinking a pink soda.

My favorite color.

He greeted her with a broad smile.

"Are you hungry?"

Nikki nodded. "Yeah. What's that you're drinking?"

"Strawberry soda. Hey, let's get out of here. What's a good place to eat?"

"Not the place I work, that's for sure. Um, let's see. Dave's Cajun is pretty good."

"Lead the way. I'll drive."

Nikki had no idea why she was getting into his BMW with him, except for the fact that he was so attentive. Fun to be with. Gentlemanly.

And he's one fine looking brother.

Nikki glanced at his profile as he drove. "Get much work done?"

"Naw, not really. Sometimes I do my best work at home. I really came out here to see you. You know that."

Nikki's chest fluttered. Yes, she had known that. Had she ever. She had doubted he drove all the way to Arcadia just to use a library on a Saturday. Isaach had come to see her, and that thought sent butterflies fluttering in her tummy.

It was a beautiful evening. The air was hot, which she loved. The top was down on Isaach's M6 convertible and she enjoyed the weather. Felt relaxed. Trustful.

I'm not sure why.

"You still have classes?"

"Yes," Nikki said. "But just a practicum meeting. It meets every other week. It's for student teachers to get together and gripe about what's going on."

"You have any gripes?"

"Not yet. I feel like I haven't really started, but that'll change next week."

"You teaching?"

"Yes. That's the plan. Turn right on Stonehill."

Isaach maneuvered his BMW around the corner. She admired his lean muscular arms resting on the steering wheel. He'd dressed differently today. Instead of his usual coordination, he wore a white muscle tee shirt, which showed off his hard, smooth chest, and a pair of blue athletic shorts.

"Looks like we're here."

Her eyes darted from his physique to the restaurant. "Oh, yeah, that's it."

He led her inside. They were seated at a table against the wall, away from the loud clatter. Nikki didn't eat out much as her budget didn't allow for it. But she enjoyed the food and hoped Isaach would as well.

"What do you recommend?"

"Crawfish," Nikki said. "It's the only thing I've ordered here."

"I love crawfish."

"Me, too. I drive to Shreveport for Mud Bug Madness."

"I'm there every year." Isaach looked at the menu.

Nikki took a deep breath. She was not completely comfortable hanging out with a student, or at least someone who would be her student next week. She tried to forget that for tonight. They were just two Arcadia College students going out to eat.

Yeah, right.

A waiter approached them. "Can I get you anything to drink?"

"Coke," Isaach said.

Nikki remembered he wasn't yet twenty-one.

What am I doing with a teenager?

"Sprite."

The waiter looked like someone she had probably seen on campus. He had long hair pulled back in a ponytail and just a touch of acne.

"I'll get that right to you," he said before he disappeared.

Issach sat back in his seat. "You get out much?"

Nikki hesitated. "What do you mean?"

"I mean get out of that dorm much."

"Here and there," Nikki said.

"What's it like?"

"What do you mean?"

"Living in a dorm. Having a roommate. Stuff like that."

"It's cool. My roommate is the best because she's never there. I get all the privacy I need." Nikki wasn't so sure she should have said that. She didn't want to sound like she was inviting him over. That they had all the time they wanted to be alone.

"That's what's up."

"It only sucks when she hogs the bathroom."

Isaach laughed. Nikki liked the way his whole face lit up. The luminous almond eyes. Pristine white teeth. Angular face. A young man who seemed to enjoy her company. That was a good start. It also didn't hurt that he was so damn sexy.

She darted her eyes around the room, suddenly fearful

someone could spot them together. But who? No one from Grayson High ever came out to Arcadia College. Except Isaach.

The waiter placed their drinks down. "Ready to order?"

Isaach glanced at Nikki.

"Crawfish étouffée," Nikki said.

"Same." Isaach closed his menu, took Nikki's from her and handed them to the waiter.

His gaze sent tingles through her lady parts. So daring. So tempting.

"So why are you taking a class here if you're not sure where you're going to go next year?"

"Try some new shit." He grinned.

Nikki smiled. "Oh, really?"

"Sure," Isaach said. "I'm nineteen. I shoulda been in college by now. I wanted to try it out."

"How do you like it so far?"

"Hard to tell from just a couple of weeks of class. What about you? You're nearly done."

If only I can get through this semester.

"It's okay. Lots of lazy students here, though. That's a big turnoff. We were assigned projects to work on as a group and nobody wanted to do anything."

"What will you do after you finish this year?"

"Get a full-time teaching job. Hopefully closer to home. Not that I can stay in the dorm, so I guess home is wherever I land."

"Where might that be?"

"I don't know yet. I was going to look around here first,

but I do want to see what's out there."

"Why English?" Isaac sipped his Coke.

"I like teaching all the fun stuff like personification, foreshadowing, author's purpose, metaphors."

"The fun stuff." Isaach smiled. "Gotta hand it to you, you know what you like."

Nikki wasn't sure if she should read into that comment or not. He didn't seem to be making any implications. But she'd been making enough implications of her own. Every furtive glance she gave him. Selecting an outfit to wear. Being so bold as to text him.

The waiter brought the crawfish étouffée, and Nikki dug into it. Predictably, it was as delicious as ever.

"This is fuckin' amazing," Isaach said. "Oh, my bad. Excuse my language."

"You must get good crawfish in Portsmith."

"Yeah, there are a few places."

Why am I sitting here with a high school senior?

Sure, she was with another Arcadia College student. It would be so innocent to look at it that way. But realistically, she was with a nineteen-year-old twelfth-grader whom she taught Senior English to at Grayson High School. Her knees trembled.

"I want you to, you know, relax."

How does he know?

Nikki gazed at Isaach. "What do you mean *relax*?"

"Aren't you a lil' tense?"

"Yes, I guess I am."

Nikki hadn't been out on a real date in some time. She'd

worked so hard on her college courses and pulled so many doubles at her job, there was little time left for men. Isaach was polite, well mannered, and beautiful. Not much else to ask for.

"I'm sorry, I didn't mean to call attention to it. I just want you to have a good time."

Nikki nodded. "I am having a good time, Isaach. No doubt. I need to do more stuff like this."

"You've got a tough job—you're on your feet all day."

"Day and night," Nikki said.

"What do you do for fun?"

What does he mean by that?

Nikki pursed her lips and her gaze wandered to the ceiling. "That's a hard one. School full-time, work full-time, not much fun time left."

"That's why you deserve a break tonight. What's there to do around here if you did have the time?"

She played with the straw in her soda glass. "Hmm, let's see. There's a movie theater not too far from here. There's also a roller skating rink for those who are well coordinated. The Grill is one of the only places you can hear live music that doesn't serve alcohol."

"Half the campus is under the age of twenty-one, so that makes sense. Would you like to go there?"

Nikki smiled. "Let's check it out."

Okay, so now I'm really taking charge.

Could have had dinner and called it a night. But no. Now the date just got extended, and there'd be no telling what could happen next. She wiped her palms with her napkin under the table.

The Grill was buzzing but not too crowded, and they managed to get a cozy table for two. The group came from Atlanta on a tour along Interstate 20. They announced they had played Grambling and Monroe the two previous evenings.

Isaach ordered coffee for both of them. Nikki wasn't sure she needed the caffeine, but the place did have good coffee. It was a local roast.

The group performed a set of hip-hop songs and the lively music stimulated her. It'd been too long since she'd gotten out and done something fun. She was accustomed to working hard for whatever she wanted, like her car and tuition, and she often let her recreation and leisure time slide.

They announced their last song and, after they finished, received thunderous applause. Nikki glanced around the room. The crowd had grown to standing room only since they'd arrived.

"We'll be in Bossier City and Shreveport the next two nights. Then we hit Marshall, Longview, Tyler, and Dallas. Spread the word!"

Isaach and Nikki filed out of The Grill.

"What did you think?"

"They're going places." Isaach paused. "Places like Bossier, Shreveport, Marshall—"

Nikki laughed. "No, what did you really think about them?"

"They're good. They're gonna make their mark in this industry one way or another."

Nikki nodded.

"Wanna take a walk?"

"Sure," Nikki said. Her heart fluttered in her chest, and the crickets hopped in her stomach. There was an excitement about this young man. An excitement she hadn't experienced with a boy in quite some time.

The campus had plenty of land and walkways, and they roamed around in the warm night air. Issach put her at ease with his laidback demeanor.

"You've worked hard for what you got."

Nikki wasn't sure if Isaach meant that as a question or a statement. "Yes."

"You bought your own car?"

"Yes, paid cash for it."

"The whole thing?"

"Um, it's like over a dozen years old. It didn't cost that much. Besides, I don't believe in car notes."

"Why not?"

"Why go into debt over a car?"

Isaach nodded. "I see your point. Tuition?"

"I got it covered. I mean, I did get some scholarships and stuff like that, but I'm responsible for the bill. That's where student loans come in."

Isaach was quiet for a moment. "I think I can learn from you."

Nikki knew he didn't mean in the classroom. "How so?"

"I need to do something on my own. My parents bought my car. They pay for my class."

"Do you still live at home?"

"Yeah," Isaach said. "That's another thing I'd like to change."

"One step at a time."

"Okay, what's the first step?"

"Get a job."

Isaach shrugged. "I'm not sure what kind of job I would get. I know what my career plans are, get an MBA, go into some kind of business. But in the short term, I don't know."

"You can get anything for now, I mean, just to get some money in your pocket."

"I haven't really looked into it."

Isaach grew quiet for a moment. Nikki was touched he revealed so much of himself. He clearly came from a good family who provided for him. He wasn't bragging. Quite the opposite, he sounded almost embarrassed that he had everything handed to him.

"Are there resources at Grayson?"

"Mrs. Ramos puts together a job fair every spring. Then there's some sort of community outreach to businesses. I haven't taken the class yet."

"Maybe you should."

"Yeah, I could sign up for it next semester. Environmental science is only one semester, so I'll have an opening to fill."

"I'm glad you have a goal to work toward. I think getting a job is a good first step."

"When did you start working?"

"When I was sixteen."

"How old are you now? If you don't mind me asking."

"Twenty-one."

"Wow. Have you had your first drink?"

"I got totally plastered on my birthday, and that was enough for me. I don't recommend it."

"But that's what everybody does."

"It didn't help that all my friends were already twenty-one and insisted on taking me out. You're nineteen?"

"Yeah, I was held back a grade, but it was when I first started school."

"We're almost the same age."

"Yeah, except you're a senior in college, and I'm a senior in high school."

"With one foot in the door of a college."

They reached Nikki's dormitory.

"Thank you, Isaach. I had an awesome time. It was just what I needed tonight."

"Thank you for seeing me."

Isaach wrapped his arms around her. Her face pressed against his chest and she felt his beating heart. His strong arms and tight hug sent a surge of heat through her. He squeezed her firmly, and it comforted her. It was probably his way of thanking her for the talk.

Isaach released her and brushed his hand along her hair. "Good night, Nikki." He bent over and kissed her on the forehead. "I had a great time with you."

"I had a great time with you." Nikki repeated his words, slightly dazed. When he held her in his arms, she didn't want him to let go. She wanted him to hold her tighter. His touch sent waves of excitement through her body. He didn't try to make a move on her sexually, yet her body responded as though aroused. Aside from dating Craig the asshole for her first two years of college, she hadn't done much with guys since.

With Isaach, it was like she'd just made a new friend. Walking and talking with him, it was as though they'd known one another for years. As he walked away, she already had thoughts of seeing him again.

**

Isaach hadn't wanted her to feel the erection he got from holding her close to him. Her soft body against his muscular frame made his dick swell. She smelled good, too. He loved a woman who smelled good.

He texted DaShon. *U up?*

He texted back. *Chillin. U comin' thru?*

Isaach texted, *On the road now.*

DaShon probably had a few people chillin' at his place. He usually did on the weekends. He opened his door to anyone on the weekends.

But Isaach's mind was on Nikki, and he likely wouldn't sleep. He'd revealed so much to her tonight. Personal stuff that he hadn't really discussed with anyone. At least not much. Not in depth.

Nikki brought it out of him. She was cool people. But more than that, someone he respected.

And here he was at DaShon's to see what's up and take his mind off pining over his teacher.

The music filtered into the driveway when Issach pulled in. It wasn't loud, but he recognized it as an old

Chamillionaire track. One of his favorites among old-school music.

He entered the crib and a few bruthas nodded to him. One of them offered him a beer, but he shook his head. He'd drunk before, but he wasn't in the mood for that. He just wanted to chill and wind down before heading home. He was grateful his parents had released his curfew when he turned eighteen. They'd strictly enforced it when he was still a minor.

He sat on the sofa and sank into the worn cushions. DaShon's friends were a chill group. They'd probably watch a movie and call it a night.

"'Sup," DaShon said, having a seat next to Isaach.

"'Sup."

"Where were you at when I texted?"

"Watching a new band. Good stuff."

"You okay?"

"Sure," Isaach said. "Just tired. Long day."

DaShon's head cranked toward the window. "Let's see who this is."

Isaach remained on the sofa. Comfortable.

A few people strolled in, and he saw someone who suddenly made his neck bristle. It was Siera. From the glazed look on her face, he assumed she'd been drinking. It wasn't hard for anyone underage to find someone to ply him or her with liquor.

What he found odd was that Siera, always a homebody, had suddenly become social. One of the guys she was with handed her a beer. That wasn't right. Not at all.

"She's only eighteen." Isaach got up from the sofa. Either they didn't hear him or chose to ignore him.

"Siera."

She looked in Isaach's direction. A faint smile formed over her face. "What you doin' here?"

"Nothing. I'm just leaving. Can I give you a ride?"

Suddenly one of the guys she'd showed up with paid attention. "She's with me."

"That's cool. I'm only offering her a ride home."

"She has one."

Isaach gazed at Siera. "You want to come with me?"

"After I finish my beer."

That put him in an awkward situation. He didn't want to interfere, but at the same time, he knew Siera wasn't a drinker. "I think you already did."

The corner of her mouth curled up. "Since when you so interested in what I do?"

"I'm not. I just want to see that you get home safely."

"She will," the other guy said.

Isaach didn't know him, and didn't really care to at the moment.

"I gotta pee." Siera disappeared into the bathroom.

Isaach clenched his fists. He wasn't looking for trouble, but he wasn't about to see her get taken advantage of. And that was exactly what was about to happen. His heart raced.

I've got to get her out of here.

"Isaach, come here," DaShon said.

Isaach glanced around the crib, then joined DaShon in the kitchen.

"What's up with that?" DaShon asked.

"She's only eighteen and I doubt she can handle liquor."

"Yeah, but man, you know how it looks."

"I know," Isaach said. "The guy's gonna think I'm muscling in on his turf. I'm not. And I don't care how it looks. This is a safety issue."

DaShon nodded and squeezed Isaach's shoulder. "Go to your car. I'll see if I can get her out to you. It'll be smoother that way. You don't wanna drag her outta here and start something."

"I see what you mean," Isaach said.

He went outside to his car and waited, grateful he'd parked where he had. The car that Siera had ridden in was parked so close to another, it apparently had put a few dings in the other car's doors when they'd gotten out.

A few minutes later, DaShon walked Siera out of the house. She was quiet until she saw Isaach.

"I'm not going with him."

DaShon put his hands on her shoulders. "You're underage. The people who brought you here don't respect that. So you can't stay here, I'm sorry. Isaach is going to take you home."

DaShon opened Isaach's passenger door. Siera looked from one young man to the next then got into the car. DaShon helped her with her seatbelt and closed the door.

"See you later," DaShon said.

"Thanks."

Isaach started the engine and rolled out of there before Siera could be missed.

"I knew this was gonna happen," Siera said.

"What?"

"You were gonna come back to me." Siera placed her hand on his crotch. He carefully removed it. "I don't wanna wait till we get home." Siera put her hand back on him and rubbed his bulge. He removed it again.

"I'm driving," he said, but he knew it was only a stalling excuse. He wasn't interested in her whether he was driving or not.

"I'm gonna suck your cock." Siera reached into his athletic shorts and pulled out his dick. She leaned over, and he slammed on the brakes. Her head banged against the steering wheel.

"Damn it!" He stuffed his dick back into his pants and got out of the car. He opened the passenger door and undid her seat belt. "Get in the back."

She didn't move. "You never had a problem with me sucking it before."

He bent over and put his face close to hers. "Make me say it again."

She laughed. "Okay, I'll let you drive." She slid out of her seat and got into the back.

"Buckle up," he said.

He got back into the driver's seat and drove her home. When they reached her place, he led her to her door.

"Lock your door, Siera, and get some sleep. Don't answer it if anyone comes by."

"I'm gonna suck your cock." She dropped to her knees and reached for his shorts.

"No, you're not." He walked back to his car.

"So who is suckin' it?" Siera yelled. "LaTanya? Bernice? Suzanne?"

Isaach turned the key in the ignition.

"Sabrina? Mavis? LaSonya?"

He backed out of her driveway.

"Jacqueline? Sharon? Christine?"

As he drove away, he hoped she'd gone inside and hadn't bothered her neighbors.

CHAPTER SEVEN

Nikki carefully read through unit one of Senior Applications in English. It all started to make sense to her. The unit was basically about forming good study skills, note taking, and research. She had spent the past three years of college doing just that, and now she had to craft a week's worth of lesson plans. It was a lot of work, and she nearly used up all the ink on her printer. But at least now she felt more confident in her abilities to teach.

Isaach is a gentleman.

As much as she concentrated on her work, Isaach's magnetic pull still couldn't be resisted. The way he'd held her last night was one of the most affectionate and warm gestures she'd received from a man. What would it be like to be held in those arms all night?

Fifth period class tomorrow. Not the best place for them to interact, as they'd already discussed. But last week Nikki could hardly take her gaze off him.

"What are you doing?" Carla breezed through the door.

"Lesson planning. What are you doing here?"

"It's my dorm room, remember?" Carla pointed a finger at herself. "Roommate."

"What's going on with Mr. Wonderful?"

"Some family thing with his mama. I don't need that drama."

Nikki turned back to her laptop. She had to turn in these lesson plans to either Mrs. Ramos or Miss Paulson. Actually, she doubted she'd get much support from Paulson and didn't need it. She could handle this classroom on her own.

"You wanna do something?"

"No," Nikki said. "I have work to do."

"Guess you were too busy last night to get any work done."

Nikki looked away from the screen. "What's that supposed to mean?"

"Someone saw you at The Grill last night with that FLB. Who is he?"

"FLB?"

"Fine lookin' brutha."

"Oh, he's a student in the business school."

"And?"

"No *and*, we just went to The Grill for coffee and to hear the band."

Carla nodded. "Yeah, right."

"But you're right. He is one fine lookin' brutha." Nikki hoped her cheeks wouldn't turn pink in front of Carla.

"So what's going on with you two?" Carla's voice went up an octave, and her expression had become more animated. Her eyebrows danced.

"Nothing. We just met."

"I've done plenty with someone I've just met." Carla plopped down on the bed and hugged her pillow, a salacious grin stretched across her face.

"I'm sure you have."

"Business student, huh?"

"Yes."

"What year?"

Nikki froze. "First. I think."

"Ohh, Nikki. I had no idea you liked 'em young."

"I don't. He's just…"

"What?"

"An FLB, like you said. A nice man. Charming. Respectful."

Carla shifted her position on the bed. "You're not worried?"

"About what?"

"You know." Carla blinked a few times. "What the kids will look like."

"What kids?"

"The kids you'd have with a FLB."

Nikki couldn't believe Carla had gone there. Was she prejudiced? Her ears burned. "You're kidding, right?"

"Well, I think of those things." Carla waved her hand as though brushing it off. "I mean, I don't really. But Mark sure does."

"He said something?"

"Well, I told him."

Nikki shook her head. "Unbelieveable."

"So, what'd you do?"

"Nothing. Just went to The Grill. End of story." Nikki was incensed but didn't want to show it. She should have known it was Carla's boyfriend's prejudice and not her own.

Carla frowned. "So you're just gonna stay here and work?"

"Yes."

"Okay, I won't bother you."

Nikki wasn't bothered by Carla, but rather by the prospect of facing tomorrow. It would be her first full day of teaching, and she had four long periods to get through. Also that gave her a longer break, and it made for a lot of class time to fill. When she was in school, class periods were about forty-five minutes. At Grayson, they were seventy-five. The trimester system was an adjustment.

Nikki's high school had been quite different. She'd been on the semester system with shorter classes. This was more like college, but maybe that was the point. A lot of high schools tried to focus more on the college experience.

Fifth period.

Isaach. By this point, it was safe to say the chemistry between them was obvious. She had to ensure it remained less noticeable. More specifically, she needed to hide that she was so attracted to him.

All six foot four of him.

She looked forward to seeing how the day went without Paulson's watchful eyes. Presumably, she or someone else would have to come into the classroom to do periodic observations. Otherwise, Nikki hoped they left her alone.

Isaach.

Nikki tried to focus on the computer screen but kept seeing his handsome face with its strong features and captivating grin. He must be a magnet for the girls at Grayson High School.

"Hungry?" Carla asked. She had her earbuds on and was bobbing her head to something.

Nikki shook her head. "No."

"I'm gonna run out and get something." Carla waved and left the dorm room.

Nikki wondered when Carla ever got any schoolwork done. But Nikki was grateful for Carla's friendship. Even though Carla wasn't around much, she always tried to include Nikki in lunches, activities, and whatnot. The only thing Nikki didn't join Carla on was shopping sprees. Nikki seldom had the extra spending money.

Someday.

Nikki hadn't been all that social in high school. She couldn't bring any of her friends home due to where she lived and her mother's eccentricities. Not that she had many. Once she'd started working, her social life had faded into the background.

The trill of Nikki's mobile phone went off. The text said, *I had a great time with you last night.* She texted back, *Same here.* High schools generally forbade students and teachers to text, but technically, they'd met on the Arcadia College campus.

He's thinking about me.

**

Isaach's tall, lean frame glistened with sweat. He shot some hoops with DaShon during Monday morning boys' athletics, his first period class. Coach Williams worked with the group at the other end of the court, and Isaach had negotiated for him and DaShon to earn some free time.

"How's it going?" DaShon asked.

"Good."

"So when do I meet her?"

"Who?"

"The girl you left Siera for."

"Whoa, I didn't break up with Siera to see someone else. I ended it because it was going nowhere."

"Wait. You not with a girl now?" DaShon looked puzzled.

"No." He wasn't prepared to talk about Nikki with anyone at Grayson High.

"That's not like you," DaShon said.

Isaach gave him a look. His friend was kinda, sorta right. Isaach always had a girl because women were attracted to him. There were other reasons, too, as he was easily tempted by a beautiful girl.

"Maybe I need a break," Isaach said.

"Um, try again." DaShon knew him too well.

"You know, I got that college course. That's a lot of work on top of my schoolwork."

"Okay, I'm seeing the picture now. You dumped the high school girl for a college girl. Excuse me, I mean college young woman." He chuckled.

Isaach grinned, not sure if he wanted to respond or not.

79

Talking about Nikki to anyone at Grayson could be dangerous right now and jeopardize her student teaching position. Gossip ran rampant in this town.

"Madison, come here."

Isaach knew that gravelly voice. It was Mr. Da'Trin, school security.

"What's that about?" DaShon asked.

"Don't know." He walked over to Mr. Da'Trin.

"Isaach, I've known you since you were a freshman. I know you come from a good family. A young lady made a complaint you been talking stuff about her."

"Don't tell me. Let me guess. Siera."

"Yes."

"Broke up with her. That's all that's about."

Mr. Da'Trin nodded. "I got it, Isaach."

He watched Mr. Da'Trin walk away, then he returned to DaShon.

"Wassup?" DaShon asked.

"Bullshit," he said. "Nothing I'm gonna worry about."

Coach Williams blew his whistle, signaling the boys to head to the locker room.

"How did you get your job?"

DaShon looked at Isaach. "Um, applied for it."

"How?"

"What do you mean?"

"Call 'em up? Fill out an application? Walk in?"

"They have a kiosk set up in the front of the store. I just sat down and filled it out. Or you can do it online from any computer. Why'd you ask?"

"Dunno. Never did it before. Might give it a try."

"You? Work?"

"Yeah."

"I know you've done a lot of volunteer stuff but it's not like you're hurting for money."

"That's not the point. I mean, I'm gonna work and have a career and all that. I just thought I should look into getting something now."

"Why now?"

Isaach shrugged. "Maybe feel more independent."

"That's a big step for you."

He wasn't sure how to take DaShon's comment. It was true that Isaach got everything he needed from his family. Perhaps things had come a little too easily for him and it was time to work for what he needed. Applying for a job might be a good step in that direction.

**

The bell rang to signal the close of first period, and Nikki sat down, exhausted. She'd been on her feet for the lesson, trying to follow her plan as best as possible.

"Who's ever pulled an all-nighter?" Nikki had asked that question to open the lesson. Curiously, none had. Perhaps they didn't know what they were getting into if they intended to go to college next year.

She remained on her feet during direct instruction, then again during guided practice. For independent practice, she monitored the rows of students. She was alone. Nosy Miss Paulson was out of the room and on to another assignment.

"What are we doing today, miss?" asked Rafael, the first student to bounce into the room for second period.

"Work."

"Good, I like work."

Nikki wasn't certain if he was serious or trying to be sarcastic. She had to be cautious how she responded to some of these kids. Most of them did not appreciate sarcasm, so she couldn't really give it back.

"Good morning, miss." She wondered if they remembered her name. The thought occurred to her that she hadn't written it on the board. She picked up the dry erase marker and wrote Ms. M—. She froze for a moment and stared at the letter M. She quickly erased it and wrote Dayton.

A shiver ran through her body.

Why did I just write M?

She faced the class as the rest of the students filed in. Second period moved more smoothly, as she taught the same lesson. Her first two periods were practically identical in terms of the functioning level of her students.

When third period rolled around, she was grateful for lunchtime. Once again, she'd forgotten to bring something and ventured into the cafeteria to sample Grayson High's menu.

She didn't move fast enough. When she got to the cafeteria, the students were already lining up. She joined the line.

"Miss Dayton." Isaach stood significantly ahead of her in line. He indicated for her to come to him.

She cautiously approached.

"Teachers are allowed to cut ahead of students." He gestured with his arm for her to stand in front of him.

"Thank you." Nikki stood in front of him and a heat radiated through her body. Her heartbeat increased being this close to him, and she cursed herself for doing it. She should have kept her place in line.

"How's your day going?" His strong and deep voice was so sexy. It reverberated through her like a beat from a good song.

"Fine," she said without turning around. With his powerful presence, she didn't dare face him. She feared he'd notice her cheeks burn. Her face blush. Her forehead glow.

"I'm looking forward to my favorite class today." A voice that could unwrinkle linen.

"Can't imagine what that is." Nikki caught herself being sarcastic.

"You know how much I love fifth period," Isaach purred. "Are you working tonight?"

She shook her head.

"I have my college class tonight. Can I see you after?"

A wave of heat rushed through her. The beating of her heart spiked, and her ears buzzed. She didn't know what to say. Seeing him again off this campus was so alluring. So tempting. She couldn't stand this close to him at Grayson. The effect he had on her was too dangerous.

"Sure," she said, her voice almost a whisper.

"That's twice I get to look forward to seeing you today." He spoke in a low tone.

She was grateful he had a sense of discretion. Her heart palpitated as she approached the serving line. She needed to get away from him before she called attention to herself.

Between the pizza and the beef, she chose pizza. Isaach leaned over, and his hot breath blew against her ear. "See you fifth period."

Dizziness hit her as she grabbed her salad and fruit cup. She handed four dollars to the cashier and hurried toward the teachers' lounge.

There were few people in the room.

"Are you okay?" There was a gentleman sitting down she hadn't seen on campus before.

"I'm fine. Why?"

"You look a little flushed."

"It's nothing."

"Devon Jackson. I'm the football coach. They also make me teach math. I guess I gotta do it to earn that check." He laughed.

She didn't. "Which grade?" She didn't really care but just said it to say something.

"Ninth. Algebra I."

She nodded. She was more interested in her pizza than his attempts at conversation.

"What do you do here?"

She really wished he hadn't asked. "Student teacher."

He nodded and went back to scarfing down his beef. Nikki wasn't in the mood to chat. She'd just gotten caught with a flushed face after her encounter with Isaach. Worse, she was certain her panties were moist.

CHAPTER EIGHT

Isaach moved through the serving line, grateful he chose to wear underwear today. Otherwise, his big boner would be prominently displayed through his thin athletic shorts. If this was the effect Nikki Dayton had on him, he had to be careful.

He joined DaShon, already seated.

"'Sup."

"'Sup."

Before Isaach put the first bite of food in his mouth, he asked, "So how often do you get paid?"

DaShon dropped his fork with a piece of beef speared on it. "That shit still on your mind? No *how are you? How's your day goin*?"

"Oh, that's wassup."

"That's what's not up." DaShon shook his head. "What has gotten into you?"

Isaach turned away. "It was just a question."

DaShon didn't say anything else.

At the end of the day, fifth period was rough. Isaach

didn't know it was going to be this bad. He could not take his gaze off Nikki and concentrate on the lesson. It had reached the point where he remained erect throughout the class. It strained against his shorts, begging for relief.

Each time she glided up the row, the pressure built against his clothing. He needed to get with her tonight and find out if she was going through the same thing. Well, not exactly the same thing. But similar feelings. He shifted in his chair and tried to keep his groin under the desk and out of sight.

"Are you okay?" It was the girl seated next to him.

"Fine."

"You keep moving."

He ignored her. If he said anything more, it would just encourage her to keep questioning him. He'd seen her in other classes and she was like that. He needed this class to be over with so he could get out of here before he exploded in his shorts.

When class ended, he nodded to Nikki on his way out but said nothing. He had her number; he would text her later, after his Arcadia class. He debated whether or not he had time for a cold shower before making the drive to the college.

Dayum.

He wasn't sure what his fifth period class was about. He would have to get the notes from someone.

Or ask Nikki for private tutoring.

He needed to pay attention and find a way to not be distracted by her. Otherwise, he would never make it through the semester. Something needed to happen so he knew where he stood with her. They'd had a great time the other night. There had to be some potential there. It was unusual for him to experience this much intensity over a woman he barely knew. He needed to be with her tonight.

He hopped into his car and got a text. It always seemed to happen that way. As soon as he got behind the wheel, his phone went off. He glanced at his phone. *Wanna watch a movie?*

This was evidence. He had to save this text in case Mr. Da'Trin asked him any more questions. Siera was telling Da'Trin one thing and yet still hadn't let go. Isaach looked forward to getting away from the high school bullshit and moving on to college.

He made a mental note to ask Nikki about filling out job applications. DaShon seemed annoyed by his questions. By the time he reached Arcadia College, his big boner had finally gone down.

**

Nikki sat at her desk. Fifth period had ended long ago and the last student filed out, but she hadn't moved. Isaach's presence in the room had overpowered teaching and learning. As she'd monitored the classroom, more than once she'd gone light-headed from the chemistry between them.

At Grayson High School, Isaach was the student, and she was the teacher. She kidded herself if she thought seeing him at Arcadia College was any different. If she knew what was good for her career, she'd avoid him. Anywhere.

"You okay, miss?" Mr. Da'Trin's voice trailed from her doorway.

"Yes, I'm fine."

"You finding your way around the school okay?"

She couldn't determine if he was giving her a bit too much attention or if he was just doing his job. "Yes, I am."

"Good to know. Holler if you need anything."

"Thanks."

Da'Trin was the security guard, yet he seemed to be a big brother figure to many of the students on campus. Many of them chatted with him in the cafeteria the few times she'd been in there.

She looked over the students' work samples. Her lesson was a fairly simple one on split page note taking. Unfortunately, she didn't think they'd been engaged. She had to work harder on grabbing their attention and keeping it.

Of course, much of that was her fault. She'd spent her energy on trying to avoid looking at Isaach. And it wasn't just his good looks, or else his allure wouldn't be so powerful. She regretted that she'd agreed to see him tonight.

She stuffed the papers in a folder and packed up. Hanging out at Grayson High any longer wouldn't improve her concentration. As she walked down the stairs, she spotted two students making out in the stairwell. They broke apart when they saw her, but she ignored them. She didn't have time to play stairway monitor. That was Da'Trin's job.

"Have a good night, miss."

There he is again.

Da'Trin stood by the doorway. Nikki nodded but said nothing. She hoped he wasn't going to become one of those annoying security guards who tried to get into everyone's business. She'd had one of those at her high school and he was a royal pain in the butt.

She got into her old car. It took a few turns of the ignition to get it started. That momentarily worried her, but as long as it got her from point A to point B, she was satisfied.

The mission for today was to pick up a few food items and head over to her mother's house. Calling it a house was a misnomer. It was actually a trailer in a rural area outside of Arcadia. Depressing didn't even begin to describe it.

Nikki braced herself before knocking on the door. As soon as she walked in, she'd become engulfed in cigarette smoke.

"It's open." The voice was hoarse.

When Nikki went inside, her mother sat at a small card table, writing on lined notebook paper.

"Hi, Mom." Her heart sank. Coming here was always painful. A reminder of the past. A reminder of where she'd come from and how hard she'd worked to put it all behind her.

"Hi, honey, what'd ya bring me?"

"I thought you might need some food."

"Oh." Her mother sounded disappointed.

Nikki placed the bag on the counter, although there was barely any space. Cluttered with unwashed dishes. None of them looked like they were from today. Dry and crusty. Her stomach lurched. She found it hard to believe her mother lived this way. Which meant, at one time, so had Nikki.

The curtains, yellowed from cigarette smoke, dangled from a bent rod. A television flickered, but the sound was muted. The silence of a lonely life.

Nikki sat across from her mother on a folding chair.

"What are you doing?"

"Writing letters. I write letters to men in prison. It passes the time for me and it brightens up their day."

Nikki frowned. "Do they ask you for money?"

"No, darlin'. Besides, what would I send them?" Her mother laughed, followed by a fit of coughing. Nikki studied the deeply etched lines in her mother's face, even though the woman was only in her early forties.

Letters to prisoners. How did her mother describe herself to them? As a ravishing young beauty? Did she send them pictures of herself? Prisoners hardly cared. They'd make her feel like a queen if they could get something out of her.

"Have you eaten anything today?"

"Yeah, I had some toast."

A coffee mug was on the table by her stack of letters. Was there something other than coffee in it? She wasn't able to smell alcohol on her mother's breath because she wasn't sitting close enough.

"How's that job of yours going?" Her mother continued writing, with only a glance in her direction.

"Fine, plus I'm student teaching."

"So, you're getting two paychecks?"

"No, Mom, student teaching doesn't pay anything. It's like an internship."

"I wouldn't do it then." Her mother paused, her pencil poised above the paper as if deciding what to write next.

"I have to do it to graduate and get my degree."

"I wouldn't do it if they don't pay you. They're just using you for your labor."

"It's part of my program of study at the college."

"Oh, yeah, the college. They'll do just about anything to get your money."

Like men in prison.

"I'm going to earn my degree in the spring."

"And then what?"

"Get a full-time teaching job."

"You have a job."

She sighed. They'd had this conversation so many times before. Her mother thought since Nikki had a waitress job she was set for life. "I have to go, Mom."

She got up and hugged her mother. Her hair reeked of stale smoke, and she could now smell alcohol. Nikki's stomach had that empty feeling, echoing the emptiness of her mother's world.

"There's some food in the bag."

"Yeah, you said. Thanks."

"I'll see you later, Mom."

As Nikki drove to the dorm, she reflected on the value of what she had. Hard work had paid for everything. Her car, her job, and her education were all products of her working nonstop since age sixteen. If she taught her high school kids anything this year, maybe she could teach them that.

Especially Isaach.

He needed to establish some sense of independence from his family. He hadn't had to work for anything, yet he wanted to. Perhaps she could help him make that happen. But how? She was a student teacher, only a couple of years older than Isaach. But their worlds were far apart. There had to something he could learn from her.

And me from him.

When Nikki reached her dorm room, she was surprised to find Carla there. For someone with such a possessive boyfriend, she spent a lot of time in the dorm room. Carla had her earbuds on and waved at her when she walked in.

Nikki put her stuff down.

"Hey, how was your day?" Carla spoke loudly.

"Fine," Nikki said. "You don't have to shout."

Carla took the earbuds out. "What?"

"How are you doing?"

"Okay. Just killing time."

"Do you ever study? Do any schoolwork?"

Carla laughed. "You know better than to ask."

Nikki was right. Carla was one of those students who just coasted. If she passed, that was good enough for her. Nikki never wanted to be that person who settled for good enough. She worked hard to be the best she could be.

She'd always been ambitious. Hard work went into every application for tuition assistance, scholarships, and grants. Not to mention her room here at the school. She could have chosen to find an apartment, perhaps even cheaper, but she wanted that college experience for her undergraduate years.

I need a shower.

The drive back and forth to Portsmith in the Louisiana heat was enough to require a couple of showers per day. That was just an excuse. The hot water soothed her body, and she glided a bar of soap all over in anticipation of seeing Isaach later..

When his text finally came, asking, *WYD*, she texted back, *Hungry.* He responded, *I'll pick you up.*

And so it started. The palpitations of her heart. The sweat on her palms. The tingling in her loins. All because of this young man. Her student.

Nikki stepped outside into the warm night air. The sun had set and it was slightly more comfortable. After a few minutes, Isaach pulled up in his BMW.

She admired his spotless car glistening in the spotlights outside the dormitory. He clearly took good care of it, and she could learn from his example.

"How's it going?"

"Good." Nikki smiled. She was pleased to see him, even though she knew she shouldn't be.

"What are you in the mood for?"

"Pizza."

"Um, didn't you have that for lunch?"

Nikki looked at him. "And?"

"Pizza it is. Point me it the right direction."

She gave him directions to a Pizza Palace not far from campus.

He noticed what I had for lunch.

His hot breath had blown on her ear as she'd struggled to get through the line without swooning. She hadn't

93

imagined he'd noticed her lunch selection.

"How was your class?"

"It was okay," Isaach said. "I just gotta focus on keeping up with the assignments. I haven't gotten the hang of that yet."

"College is very different from high school."

"For real."

"Don't worry, you're in the right place. Senior Applications in English is all about getting ready for college." Nikki almost wished she hadn't said that. It was a reminder that she was his teacher, and he was her student as long as they were at Grayson High.

But we aren't at Grayson High tonight.

She had to put their classroom relationship out of her mind for now if she planned to enjoy his company without worrying herself into a knot. Besides, she had pizza on her mind. She needed food. She'd barely eaten her lunch at the high school.

When they arrived at Pizza Palace, she got out of the car before waiting to see if Isaach would open her door. He was gallant enough without her falling into the role of expecting it.

"What kind do you like?" Isaach asked.

"All kinds." Nikki had pepperoni for lunch, so she decided on the veggie explosion. Isaach ordered it for her, then a hamburger pizza for himself, and Cokes for them both. They took their number card and found a seat by the window.

"I had a rough day in class today," Isaach finally said.

"I thought you said it was okay?" She gazed as his face. His angular features. Deep charcoal complexion. Captivating smile.

"I meant your class. I couldn't concentrate."

"Why not? Do I suck at teaching?"

He smiled. "No. I was thinking about you the whole time."

Nikki went silent for a moment, her stomach in knots. She'd been thinking of him the whole time. Or rather, trying not to think of him.

"I had to see you tonight." Isaach touched her hand.

Fire shot up her arm at his touch. A simple touch. From a man she shouldn't be with.

Hadn't she known this would happen if they saw each other tonight? Like in line in the cafeteria today and in class. Had she not agreed to see him tonight, she would have only prolonged it.

Still, she wasn't certain what to say. She wasn't sure she could trust her attraction to him. So strong that it was almost scary.

"Am I making you uncomfortable?" he asked.

"No." She shook her head. "I was just thinking."

Overthinking.

"About?"

"What you're saying." Nikki paused, her heart racing. "I feel it, too." Her face flushed the moment the words came out.

Isaach nodded. "I know you do."

The pizza arrived and suddenly she didn't feel so hungry. She ate slowly, exchanging glances with Isaach. Shivers ran through her body. They were on the same page. She'd reached that point where there was no turning back.

After they finished their sodas, they got into Isaach's car and headed back to Arcadia College. They found a spot to pull over, and Isaach took Nikki into his arms. His large, muscular limbs pressed her close to him, and he kissed her. When their lips touched, a jolt of excitement ran through her body. Her core surged, and everything became heightened.

When his tongue met hers, her belly radiated with heat. She grabbed his large bicep and pushed her tongue against his.

No turning back now. This was the moment she'd put off. An inevitable moment.

She'd denied herself this pleasure for too long. Juggling two to three jobs for five years, her desire for independence had taken over her desire for a man. Tonight, she found all the man she needed in Isaach.

"Don't you need to get back home?" she asked.

"No."

"I thought you said you lived with your parents?"

"I'm nineteen."

His lips were only an inch or two from hers as they spoke. He kissed her again, and they sat in the car for a long time doing nothing but exploring each other's mouths. Nikki pulled away for a moment. She'd never known a man could be this good. Heat overcame her and it wasn't the weather. Her whole person filled with fire from his touch. Isaach pulled her close to him with his strong arms and rested her head against his chest.

What about tomorrow?

CHAPTER NINE

Isaach had lost track of the time. They sat in his car with his arms wrapped around her as he stroked her long red hair. They didn't speak much, and they didn't have to. They had a connection neither one of them could deny.

Nikki stirred, her eyelids droopy.

"What time is it?"

"Don't ask. You'll sleep better if you don't know." At least, that was what always worked for him. If he didn't look at the clock before he went to bed, he tended to get a better night's sleep.

"I'd better go. I have to work tomorrow."

"I know." Isaach hoped he hadn't sound flippant.

Nikki shook her head. She reached for her bag, pulled out a brush, and ran it through her hair a few times. She turned to open the door, then squeezed his hand.

"Thank you."

Isaach squeezed it back. "Thank you."

Nikki walked across the lawn to her dormitory, and Isaach stayed put until she entered the building safely. He sat there for a moment, then headed back home.

How can I feel this for her when tempted by many?

With the top down on his convertible and the warm night air against his face, it came to him. Nikki signaled a change. She was strong and independent at only twenty-one, and he could learn from her. He wanted to get to know her in a way he hadn't with other girls. They had all come too easily to him in the past.

He'd had his second date with Nikki and no sex. He hadn't dated a girl twice without sex since he was about thirteen. Funny thing was, he didn't even want it yet. His body did, but his mind told him to wait.

He'd forgotten to ask her about job applications, but that could wait. They'd reached a more important milestone tonight. That kiss was more intimate than any sexual encounter in his past. There would be plenty of time to ask her advice on jobs.

Dayum, it's late.

He'd totally lost track of the time and hadn't meant to keep her up. They'd sat in the car for hours. Hopefully, she wouldn't be sluggish at work in the morning on account of him.

When Isaac got home, he crawled right into bed. Sleep did not come easily. He wanted to be lying next to Nikki and holding her in his arms all night long.

I'll make it happen.

The next morning at school, Isaach waited in the cafeteria for the first period bell to ring. He looked around for DaShon but couldn't find him in his usual spot.

"Good morning, Isaach." Miss Paulson marched right up to him. "How's your new teacher working out?"

"Fine."

"Everything okay in the classroom?"

Isaach nodded.

"How's everything else going?" She twirled a finger through her brunette curls.

Isaach had no idea where she was headed with this. "It's going."

"If you need any help with anything, let me know. I tutor from seven forty-five to eight forty-five each morning." Paulson held his gaze before moving on.

What's that all about?

DaShon slinked up to him. "What's up with her?"

"Don't know."

"She got the hots for you."

"No, it's not that."

"I think it is. Better be careful, Isaach. You don't wanna be messin' with a teacher."

"Like you, right?"

Her behavior in the classroom had been a little odd. Isaach had attributed that to competition between her and her younger, fairer student teacher. He didn't think it had anything to do with him.

The day rolled along and he was grateful for fifth period. He was relaxed in class and even Nikki appeared to be more confident and in control. The time they'd spent time together last night eased some of the uncertainty.

After school, Isaach lingered with some of the guys when

he got a text message from Nikki. All the text said was, *Help*.

Isaach immediately texted back, *Where r u?*

Parking lot.

Isaach headed outside and found her standing by her car in the hot sun. She shielded her eyes with a hat, but her tense body language indicated she was stressed. She fidgeted and moved her whole body when she spoke.

"What's wrong?"

"Won't start."

"Pop the hood."

Nikki did as he said, and Isaach stuck his head under it.

"Be right back." He sprinted off to his car and returned with a wrench. He ducked back under the hood and tried to get the connector to stick to the battery, but it wouldn't. It had become warped from wrangling with it.

"You need a new battery connection, and most likely it needs to be rewired."

"Great. How can we make that happen?"

"Only way is to take it to a dealer or repair shop."

Nikki's expression soured. "You mean call a tow truck to take it?"

"Not really. I can probably use some tape to make it stick to get it to the shop, but I wouldn't drive it home this way if I were you."

"Sounds like I'm stuck."

"Hold up." He went back to his car and returned with some electrical tape. He wrapped the connector around the battery as best he could, but still didn't like the look of the wiring. It appeared frayed.

"Okay, start her up."

Nikki gave it a try, and the engine sputtered to life.

He leaned against her car. "Follow me. We'll get it to a shop. You can't drive back to Arcadia with it taped up like that."

She paused for a moment, looking as though about to explode, and then took a deep breath and nodded.

After they dropped off the car, Nikki joined him in his BMW.

"Now what?"

"I can take you home."

"Shouldn't we wait? He said he would try to get to it today."

"Try usually means tomorrow. But you're right. We should wait." Isaach pulled out of the lot.

**

The air conditioning helped ease her flustered state. It was a hot day, and the sun blistered. Her trusty car bought with hard-earned waitressing money had failed her. No need dwelling on that now. Nikki leaned back and tried to relax.

Isaach's car weaved down a heavily wooded street. Grand houses stood majestic off the road, houses like she hadn't seen in Portsmith. He pulled up to a massive two-story house.

"Where are we?"

"My place."

Nikki was stunned. The house could be described as palatial. Tall Grecian columns. Exquisitely manicured lawn.

Flower gardens galore. All this grandeur tucked away in an exclusive hamlet.

He opened the passenger door for her, and she couldn't take her eyes off the house. He took her hand and led her inside.

A marble winding staircase led up the second floor. The color scheme was neutral—beige, taupe, tan. Tall ceilings. Paintings. Sculptures. Nikki couldn't recall seeing anything so impressive.

"*Hola*," greeted a cheerful middle-aged woman.

"*Hola*," Isaach responded.

"*Hola*," Nikki said, because it seemed like the thing to say.

The woman disappeared into another room.

"Who was that?" Nikki asked.

"Stella. Come on upstairs."

Isaach led Nikki up the curved staircase. "Who's Stella?"

"Part of the family. She's worked for my parents since before I was born."

Nikki was beginning to form a picture in her mind. Isaach was from a well-off family. Duh. The house was huge, and she was awestruck.

"She's your maid?"

Isaach laughed. "I would never call her that. But yeah, I guess that's how she started here."

"You mean when your parents first hired her?"

"I guess."

Wow. This was how Isaach lived. Talk about the other side of the tracks. This palatial estate was light-years from the tracks.

"What do your parents do, if you don't mind my asking?"

"Dad's a doctor, mom's a dentist."

"Oh." That explained the BMW. Was his thug style of dress an attempt to camouflage that he came from means?

Then why drive a BMW?

Isaach opened a door. "Here's my room."

Nikki marveled at the size of it. He had a king bed, a desk, a media center, and a walk-in closet. The bed had been made but the closet door left open. Nikki couldn't help but peek inside. Rows and rows of quality athletic apparel and numerous pairs of athletic shoes were all neatly arranged.

Stella appeared in Isaach's doorway and placed a tray with two tall glasses on a table by the door. She slipped away without saying a word.

Isaach handed a glass to Nikki. "Iced tea."

"Thank you."

"No problem."

"And thanks for all your help."

"You wanna play a game?"

His media center had two large chairs, gaming consoles, and just about everything else. They took their glasses over and had a seat. He handed her a wireless controller and got a game going.

She wasn't much of a gamer but held her own. Finally, the stress from her car issues melted away, and she had some fun. Hopefully, her car would be ready tonight so she could avoid asking Isaach to drive her back to Arcadia.

But she had to ask him. She couldn't show up for work

at Grayson High wearing the same dress she'd worn today.

"Hey, I'm gonna take a shower." Isaach headed for the bathroom built into his bedroom. "You don't mind?"

"No, not at all," Nikki said.

After Isaach closed the door, Nikki took some time to be nosy. She stepped into Isaach's walk-in closet and scanned the sheer number of garments he had. Not to mention shoes. This young man had it all. There was a full-length mirror, bottles of cologne—although she couldn't recall picking up a scent on him—and some hats.

Back in the bedroom, she admired a display of pictures, presumably of family and friends. His desk had a laptop, some schoolbooks, notebooks, snacks and bottled water.

"Much better." When Isaach emerged from the bathroom, he wore only a towel. Droplets of water glistened all over his smooth, lean muscles. His sinewy muscles. The perfectly carved abs. His large arms, ready to engulf her. Nikki had to avert her gaze.

"Hey, you mind if I take one? I could use it."

"Sure, go right ahead. Towels in the closet, as well as soaps, shampoos, lotions, and all that."

"Thanks."

Once in the bathroom, she closed the door and sat down for a moment.

What am I doing here?

In the bedroom of one of her students. A student she'd made out with for hours in his car at Arcadia College.

With a deep intake of breath, she got up and rummaged through the closet. A large bath towel, a wash towel, and some soap should do it. And a grip on her nerves.

This is insane.

Who else could she have called? She barely knew anyone at the school. Isaach had helped her with her car before. It made sense to call him.

Or a tow truck.

She got the hot water going and took a few deep breaths.

"Did the phone ring?" Nikki had a towel wrapped around her hair but was otherwise dressed when she emerged from the bathroom. Isaach lay on his back wearing only a pair of athletic shorts.

"No, but there's still time. They don't close for another two hours."

Nikki gazed at him and that tingling sensation surged through her body. She sat at the edge of the bed, her inner core on fire. Her ears burned and nerves seared.

I'm sitting on a bed with one of my students.

He pulled her to him, and her head rested on his chest. His heart thudded against her ear, but hers raced faster than a record-breaking sprinter. How could she? With so much on the line?

"You can lose the towel. You'll probably be more comfortable."

Nikki removed the towel from her hair, and Isaach took it from her, dropping it to the floor. He guided her back to his chest. She closed her eyes and savored the moment of her cheek pressed against his smooth muscles.

Her ringtone disturbed the peaceful moment. She'd closed her eyes for a few minutes and allowed herself to forget the danger.

"Hello?"

The mechanic droned on with a long-winded explanation.

"Okay." She put down the phone. "They won't get to it tonight."

"That's okay. I'll take you back to Arcadia."

"Isaach, I still need to get to work in the morning."

"Don't think about that now." He pulled her back down to the bed, rolled onto his side, and kissed her. As soon as she felt his lips on hers, she was transported to a different place. Her senses heightened, her head started spinning, and she surrendered.

Nothing could have prepared her for the blazing heat in her core. The ache between her legs had to be soothed. And only one thing could do that. The man lying next to her in bed.

And she forgot about it all. The car, tomorrow, and everything else faded away. All she could think about was the tall young man who had captured her attention and earned her trust.

Trust.

She wasn't sure she could or should trust. It was new to her to surrender to a man so readily. He'd helped her in times of need more than once. Even if he hadn't, she wanted to be here with him in his bed.

He scooped her in his arms and rolled on top of her. She ran her hands along his strong V-shaped back. He kissed her with intensity, and she held on to him as her body raged with need. His hand reached for the buttons of her dress and unfastened the first one.

Nikki put her hand over his. "Stella."

"What about her?"

"I mean, she's still in the house, right?"

Isaach intertwined his fingers with hers. "I told you, Stella is just like family to me." He leaned down and kissed her and unfastened her remaining buttons. She played with fire. They were two consenting adults, but if anyone at either the high school or the college found out she was involved with a student, she could be in trouble.

Big trouble.

Nikki ran her hand along his closely cropped hair and hungered for more of his deep kisses. He opened her dress and moved his lips down to her breast. Another rush of heat rose through her as her nipple swelled in his mouth.

"Isaach."

"Are you okay?"

She nodded. Yeah, she was okay, as long as she was with him. She had to trust that. He put his mouth on her other breast, and she pressed her hand against the back of his head. She didn't want him to move. His hand reached between her legs, and his fingers glided into her. She arched her back, writhing from the pleasure of his touch. He devoured one nipple while his thumb caressed her nub.

"Isaach." She called his name, her voice breathy.

He sucked on her nipple and rhythmically moved his fingers and thumb. Heat raged through her core and throughout her body. Her mind was lost in a torrent of conflicting thoughts, none of which made any sense. Run. Stay. Resist. Surrender.

Wave after wave rushed through her until she cried out his name again, more loudly than before. She was transported to another place, and there'd be no turning back now. She clutched his body.

"Isaach!"

He placed his mouth over hers and filled her with deep kisses. She was on fire now and squirmed under the weight of his muscular frame. She clutched his head with both hands, eager to meet his tongue with every kiss.

Isaach pulled her dress up and rolled over to remove his athletic shorts. He kneeled on the bed with one massive thigh on either side of her, so he was hovering over her. He was completely naked now, and his erection jutted straight out at her. It was so long it didn't seem real. She reached out to touch it.

He leaned back for a minute, grabbed something, and faced her again. He unwrapped a condom and rolled it down his shaft. It stopped about three-fourths of the way down his long dick.

She touched his arm, and he leaned down to kiss her. Her tongue meshed with his, and the ache between her legs craved relief. One of his knees pressed against her leg and pushed it down. He slipped one strong arm under her waist and the other around her shoulders and slowly glided into her. She cried out and clutched his back, pulling him closer to her.

The initial discomfort of his length gave over to pleasure, and waves rippled through her. He slid deeper into her, and she surrendered to the intensity. Her body shuddered and quaked under him, and she cried out so loudly that Stella must have heard her.

Her body writhed as his pace increased. She was drenched in sweat but didn't care. She wanted Isaach, and at this moment, she had him. Endorphins exploded and her vision had become a kaleidoscope of color and light as her body shivered.

His breathing deepened, and she gripped his back as he reached his climax. She hadn't been able to shake him from her thoughts since the day she'd met him, and now he was inside her.

He pounded into her and let out a deep, guttural groan.

"Wow." Isaach collapsed on her and buried his face in her neck.

Nikki held him, and her hands slid across his moist back. He breathed heavily, and his hot breath heated her flesh even further.

His head moved and his lips were on hers again. Soft and wet, his kisses aroused her.

"Are you still worried about getting home?"

"Not even thinking about it."

"Good. I'll take you whenever you're ready."

She pulled him closer for another kiss, hardly ready.

Later, they cruised down Interstate 20. Isaach had the top down and Nikki enjoyed the calm night. He held her hand during most of the drive.

"Do both your parents work long hours?"

"Dad does. Mom doesn't, but she also doesn't come

rushing home since Dad's not there."

But you're there.

"Do you have any brothers or sisters?"

"One sister. Older. She's at Morehouse."

Unless he depended a lot on Stella, Isaach must be more independent than he let on. He certainly didn't have his parents around. Perhaps that's why they gave him everything—an attempt to compensate for not being there.

When they reached her dormitory, Isaach put the top up on his car. He walked her up to her room, and Nikki was grateful that Carla wasn't there. Nikki grabbed some bottled water out of the fridge and handed one to him.

"Thanks."

Nikki sat on the bed. She was tired for more than one reason. Tomorrow would be a very full day as she was on the schedule at the restaurant right after she finished teaching. She leaned back.

"I'll stay here tonight," Isaach said. "You know I'm not gonna fit in that bed, so I'll just stretch out on the floor."

"You don't have to do that."

"Yeah, I do. How you gonna get to work tomorrow?"

"But you need to get home."

"I'm nineteen."

"I keep forgetting that. At least send a text to your parents telling them not to worry."

"They're used to me being out all night."

Nikki wasn't sure she wanted him to venture any further on that subject. Realistically, she did need a ride to work tomorrow.

"The floor's not that clean. Take this comforter and a pillow."

Because he was so tall, it would be awkward for him to share her twin bed. She could offer Carla's bed, but he would probably refuse. Besides, she could show up at any time, knowing her.

"How are you feeling?"

"Okay."

He knelt down before her. "I want to make you feel better than okay."

Isaach pushed her dress up and kissed her sweet spot. Ripples of pleasure ran throughout her. He slipped a few fingers inside her and continued to nibble and lick on her clit. Nothing in her life had prepared her for the pleasure of his touch. Flushed with heat, she grabbed his arm and held on as her body quaked with wave after wave of rapture.

She glowed from the perspiration that had broken out all over her. Her breathing returned to a normal pace, but Isaach did not come up. He moved his face deeper between her legs and worked his tongue inside her. After she reached another climax, he turned off the lights in the room.

Nikki lay in bed for a long while, staring up at the ceiling. After some time, Isaach's deep breathing comforted her. He was real. He was here. And she had slept with him. Her student.

The damage had been done.

**

The next morning, her old clock radio jolted her from a restless sleep. She found the off switch, and she pushed her hair away from her face.

Isaach lay on the floor with the comforter wrapped around his large frame, and his head rested on the pillow. She gazed at him for a long time before speaking.

"Good morning," Nikki said.

Isaach's eyes fluttered open. Funny that he hadn't heard the music from the radio but responded to the sound of her voice.

"Mornin'," he said, rolled over, and closed his eyes again.

She was grateful that he was here. Not just here in her room but in her life. He filled a void she hadn't known she had. She let him rest as she staggered to the shower. She hadn't slept enough, and he probably needed sleep as much as she did.

Guilt consumed her. How could she have allowed a student to spend the night in her room? What would the consequences be if Mrs. Ramos or anyone at Grayson High found out? Nikki would be toast.

She got a pot of coffee going as soon as she stepped out of the bathroom. With her trusty supply of cups and lids, they'd have to drink it on the go in order to make it to school on time.

"Mmmm." Isaach rolled over again. He must've smelled the coffee.

He pulled himself up off the floor and gave her a big hug. After he carefully folded the comforter, he placed it and the pillow on the bed.

"Guess we better get goin'."

Nikki handed him a cup of coffee. "For the road."

Isaach took the cup from her and placed it down. "Gotta

use it first." He ducked as he went into the bathroom.

The ride back to Portsmith gave Nikki time to sip her coffee and focus on the day ahead. Her car would be ready by the time school dismissed, and she could head to work.

Long day.

She glanced at Isaach. His life was a series of contrasts. His father worked long hours, his mother presumably partied with her friends after work, and his older sister was away at college. He was independent in the sense that he came and went as he pleased, but he seemed to depend on his family—and Stella—for everything else.

How awkward will fifth period be?

They pulled into Grayson High's parking lot, and they weren't late.

"Thank you," Nikki said.

"Thank you." Isaach squeezed her hand.

As Nikki walked up to the entrance, she glanced up at a second floor window. Staring down at her was Sarah Paulson. The look on Paulson's face was not friendly.

Busted.

CHAPTER TEN

The day went a little strange. Isaach couldn't shake the feeling he was being watched. Miss Paulson sauntered through the cafeteria giving him a look that made him uncomfortable.

Maybe I should transfer out of fifth period.

It was a required course. If he didn't take it fifth period, he would have to juggle his whole schedule. There also could be questions from his advisor, and he wouldn't be able to justify why he wanted to rearrange his whole day. Still, he had to do whatever he could to protect Nikki's position here. If his presence in her class was detrimental, he needed to do something about it.

"Need help with anything, Isaach?" Miss Paulson hovered over him.

"Yeah, how to fill out a job application." He blurted out the words before he realized what he was saying. She had unnerved him a few minutes ago with her look, and now she caught him by surprise.

Paulson laughed. "That's easy enough. Come by my

room tomorrow morning for tutoring. Or, if it's more convenient for you, today after school."

Isaach nodded.

"I've been meaning to ask you…the spelling of your name is so unique. Where did it come from?"

"My mom named me after an actor."

"Interesting. See you later, Isaach." Paulson walked away with the speed of a sloth. Perhaps she thought it showed off her backside, which was actually kind of flat.

What was she up to? He didn't trust her tone. There'd been some tension between Paulson and Nikki in class, but that could have been because Nikki was new and it'd been her first week.

He grabbed his phone. He'd forgotten he'd turned it off at Nikki's so as not to disturb her sleep. Predictably, a slew of text messages popped up. He answered a couple from DaShon and headed to his guidance counselor.

"You'll be late for class," she said by way of a greeting. His guidance counselor was one of those administrators who always seemed bothered when a student walked into her office.

Like that's not what she's here for.

"Can I change my schedule?"

"What's the problem?" Miss Anders had never taught before and it was obvious. She didn't seem to connect well with children.

"There's no problem, I was just—"

"No." She wasn't smiling. Her manner was curt and dismissive.

"No?"

"It's the second week of school, Isaach. If there's not a problem, and I mean an urgent one, just deal with whatever you've got going on. Or whomever."

Isaach froze for a moment.

What's that supposed to mean?

He did have a reputation on campus as a magnet for girls. Perhaps she was just alluding to that. He mumbled something and left her office.

This day is wack.

When he reached boys' athletics, he found DaShon on the mat doing his warm-up exercises. That was exactly what Isaach needed to do. His body was stiff from sleeping on the floor.

"'Sup."

"'Sup. Why you late?"

"No reason."

"Yeah, right." DaShon stretched his hamstrings.

Isaach bent over. "Just had to take care of some stuff."

"Whatever, Isaach. Not my business."

"You asked."

DaShon grunted as he pushed himself to stretch farther. Isaach was fairly limber, but he had to get the kinks out of his body. "What's up with you?"

"Work. Something you know nothing about."

That stings.

"Why so cold?"

DaShon laughed. "Don't worry about it. I got jokes, that's all."

"What are you doing after school?"

"Work."

"You think I could come by and apply?"

DaShon nodded. "Sure, Isaach, you do that."

He didn't sound sarcastic, but Isaach wasn't sure that DaShon meant what he said.

**

Grateful when third period arrived, Nikki had time to sit down and rest. She'd been on her feet all morning and was exhausted. At least fourth period would bring her favorite group of kids. Then fifth period would bring Isaach.

How can I be his teacher?

It had been gnawing at her all morning, ever since she's seen Sarah Paulson glaring at her from the upstairs window. Paulson might or might not be on to them, and Nikki was not about to ruin her day with worry. She had far too much to get through today. Besides, anything Paulson might say would be suspicion alone. She had no evidence of any wrongdoing.

But Nikki feared that she and Isaach would be found out, one way or another.

I had sex with a student.

She couldn't avoid Isaach. He was in her class, plus she had to leave school with him today so she could pick up her car and get to work. Somehow, they needed to come up with a solution to the awkwardness they faced. Not to mention the conflict of interest with her position at Grayson High School.

My car.

Nikki checked her handbag. She had her emergency cash envelope on hand. She hoped there was enough in there to cover the repair. She hated pulling out the plastic to pay for anything.

Nikki had spent way too much money on her first three years of college to blow everything during her fourth. She needed this degree, this job, and her certification. All of that rested on student teaching.

This is gonna be one helluva year.

"How's it going?"

Nikki hadn't realized she'd left her classroom door open. A young woman stood in the doorway. It was the same lady she'd met in the teachers' lounge.

"Oh, it's going well. I guess. I'm sorry; I don't remember your name. I've met so many people here."

"That's okay. Sheryl Moore."

"Nikki Dayton."

"So, you took over for Paulson already?" Sheryl took a step into the classroom.

"Yeah."

"That must be a relief."

Nikki chose not to go there. "You're from Monroe, right?"

"Uh-huh. She won't be in the room much. But she still has to come in to do evaluations of you."

"So what was your impression of her?" Nikki figured there was no use changing the subject.

"Not the most warm and fuzzy person I've ever met."

Nikki laughed. "I can agree with that."

Sheryl ran a hand through her sandy blonde hair. "You know she wants to be a principal."

"For real?"

"Yeah, I think that's why she does all this extra stuff like mentoring and tutoring. She's trying to beef up her credentials."

"She looks kinda young."

"And very ambitious. You only have to teach five years before you can apply for principal jobs. She's got that."

"She needs a master's degree."

Sheryl nodded. "She got that last year. The thing you gotta watch out for with her is that she's always into everyone else's business."

"How so?"

"Nosy. Always trying to find out stuff. Sniffin' around where she shouldn't."

Nikki was still haunted by the image of Paulson staring at her this morning.

"Of course, she's got her own business to worry about." Sheryl had this look on her face that indicated she might have more to say.

"Oh?" If Nikki had any question about who was the school gossip, she'd surely just found out.

"She's been known to get a little too friendly with some of the older students. It's all rumor. Nothing ever stuck because no one filed a complaint."

Nikki wondered why Sheryl was telling her all of this. Certainly it couldn't be a warning.

Or is it?

Sheryl's words made sense. If what she said about Paulson was true, then perhaps she had picked up on something between them. That could be dangerous.

A short time later, a light rap on the door got her attention. It was Barbara, a special needs student from her fourth period class, although it was still long before class started. Barbara had a specific learning disability in reading, although she was quite high functioning otherwise.

"Miss Dayton?"

"Hi, Barbara."

"Can I talk to you for a minute?"

"Sure, come in. But shouldn't you be in your third period class?"

"This is my lunch."

Nikki nodded. "What's up?"

"The assignment from yesterday. I didn't do my best. So I rewrote it." She pulled a piece of paper from her folder and held it out. "Will you look at it?"

"Of course." Nikki was touched that the girl would take that initiative. So few students seemed interested in completing an assignment once, let alone redoing it.

By the time fifth period rolled around, Nikki fluctuated between exhaustion and nervousness. She was about to instruct a classroom full of students, one whom she'd slept with last night.

What have I gotten myself into?

As the class filed in, she tried to avoid eye contact with him, but it didn't work. She was drawn to him and found it very difficult not to look at him. Every inch of him, golden smile, massive sex appeal.

"Today, I want to talk to you about online versus campus classes. During the past three years, more than half of my classes were exclusively online. The remainder had some portion online."

They were not exactly captivated by her information.

"The reason I bring that up is that most students approach online classes thinking they're easy. They're actually harder."

Groans. Comments like, "Why's she telling us this?"

"Online classes are demanding and the tests are hard. Your study skills are every bit as important, if not more important, as with campus classes."

Isaach's gaze was on her, and as much as she tried to fight it, she felt an ache between her legs where he'd been last night. She wanted him again. She played with fire and she knew it, but he made her wet just by looking at her.

"Miss Dayton." It was a student in the front row.

"Yes?"

"Are you going to grad school?"

"That's a good question. I haven't made that decision yet. I'll probably think more about that as I get closer to my graduation."

Nikki reached over to her desk and grabbed a stack of papers. "I've made some comments on your papers." Nikki was about to pass them out when Isaach got out of his seat and approached her, hand extended.

"I'll get those for you."

"Thank you." Her face flushed.

Nikki's complexion, usually pale, must match her hair. She tried to remain composed, but the students already looked at her oddly.

This is tough.

Seventy-five minutes of this, five days a week. Nikki wasn't going to make it. Something had to be done. She couldn't be in the same room with Isaach and pretend they hadn't been intimate.

His tall, lean frame moved confidently around the room. He knew most of the students, so he passed them out far more quickly than she could have.

He looks so good.

"Today I want to go over some of the study techniques that you might find helpful for an online course."

He feels so good.

"I am going to model how you would approach an online assignment."

He tastes so good. Like spearmint.

"The assignment will be posted on Grayson's share drive and you will need to post your work to the drive."

She had become light-headed and had to stop. She clutched the edge of a student's desk and took a moment to compose herself. After a quick glance at the clock, she silently cursed how much time she had left before the bell.

"You okay, Miss Dayton?" It was the student whose desk she leaned on.

Is it obvious?

"Yes, fine," Nikki lied. She was anything but fine. Her

panties were moist, and she was about to swoon over the man she'd shared a bed with yesterday.

Isaach gazed at her intently. He must know something was up.

She had to make it through to the bell.

"May I volunteer something?" Isaach asked.

"Yes?" Nikki had no idea what he meant.

Isaach stood up. "I'm taking a class at Arcadia College now. I don't mind sharing my experiences."

"Please, go ahead." She wandered to the back of the room as Isaach went up front to the board.

She took a seat. She could feel the wetness between her legs. Isaach took over the classroom and basically taught until the bell. He shared what it was like to take a college class, shared the expectations, and outlined some things the students needed to prepare for.

He was wonderful and had the class's attention the whole time. He did a much better job than she could do considering the state she was in.

The bell finally rang, and Isaach remained behind. When the last student left, he shut the door.

"Are you okay?"

She stood. "Isaach."

He took her in his arms, and she rested her head against his chest. He rubbed her back and grabbed her butt. She moaned, and Isaach gently leaned her against the classroom wall. He kissed her and slid his hand under her dress. Fire raged through her. How could this happen here, in the classroom?

123

He explored her folds, and her body trembled. What had happened yesterday couldn't be repeated again. Too much to lose.

He rubbed her nub until her body quaked, sending spasms through her legs. Weak on her feet, she held on to him for fear she'd collapse.

His touch brought her that release she needed so badly. But what else could it bring? Charges? Dismissal? The end of her career before it started?

"Isaach, I need to get to work."

"Then we had better go pick up your car from the shop."

**

Much later, at work, Nikki could barely stand up. She needed a good night's sleep. Don worked tonight, and it didn't help that he kept asking her over and over again if she was feeling okay. She wanted to slug him but decided that wouldn't go over so well with the customers or her boss.

"Did you eat anything today?" Don asked.

"Yes." Actually, she hadn't eaten since lunch. She should have had something when she got to the diner, but had run late because of her car.

At least the vehicle had been ready when Isaach drove her to the shop.

"The turkey is good today." Don hovered around her, waiting for an answer.

"That's terrific, Don."

The diner was crowded tonight, and she didn't have time to chat. She might be able to scarf something down later, but not now. As busy at is was, Don always seemed to find time to hover around her and do nothing. Dishwashers had it made.

Isaach.

Nikki shouldn't be thinking of him while at work, but it was impossible not to. He made her melt just by looking at her. If she continued to teach with him in the class, she faced a major challenge.

"Is the turkey fresh?" The customer looked like the picky type. Nikki could spot them from the first question.

"Yes, sir, it's fresh."

Isaach was only two years younger than her, yet they were worlds apart. The hardworking middle class girl who paid for everything she had with her own labor versus the son of affluent parents who gave him everything.

Everything but attention.

With his looks and his charisma, he could probably have any girl he wanted. He was gallant in a way she didn't know a nineteen-year-old man could be. Attentive. Thoughtful. Generous. She reflected on how he'd driven her back to Arcadia and spent the night so she would have a ride to work the next morning.

Considerate.

Nikki still had to solve the proximity problem. Being in the same room with him was intoxicating. The fact that the same room happened to be a classroom was dangerous.

There were too many people at Grayson High who were nosy. Sarah Paulson was number one on that list. She was sniffing around for something. Mr. Da'Trin seemed to take too much of an interest in what was going on at the school. The only person who seemed to mind her own business was Mrs. Ramos, the principal.

Sheryl Moore seemed nice enough. She might have a loose tongue, but Nikki got the impression that Sheryl meant well. The one to watch out for was Paulson.

What is she up to?

CHAPTER ELEVEN

"Good morning, Isaach. I'm glad you could come." Sarah Paulson purred like a kitten. Gone was her usual dowdy style of dress, replaced with a bright red blouse and black skirt.

Why am I here?

She'd offered to help him during her tutoring session, but Isaach had a feeling in his stomach that something wasn't right.

"Good morning, Miss Paulson."

"Sit down, Isaach. Over here, at this computer." She indicated a chair right next to hers, at the bank of computers located along the wall of the classroom. Curiously, no other students were here.

Why did she schedule her tutoring sessions so early? Maybe because the school was quiet? There'd be fewer distractions.

"I did my homework last night, Isaach."

"Huh?"

"I searched the net to find out who you were named after. That big, brawny beefcake Isaach DeBankole."

127

Tempted to roll his eyes, Isaach refrained. He kinda wished he hadn't told her he was named after an actor.

"Now tell me again what you needed help with?" Her smile lacked sincerity.

"Job applications."

"Okay, what type of job did you want to apply for?"

He had no idea. DaShon worked in a store, so perhaps that was a good start.

"Retail."

"Good. There are plenty of retail stores in Portsmith. Let's take a look at some."

He didn't like her tone. It was almost condescending. He wasn't an elementary school kid who didn't get division. He was a grown man trying to do something constructive.

"Have you applied online before?"

He shook his head. "No, ma'am."

"Have you worked before?"

"No, ma'am."

Paulson's hand rested on his exposed thigh. "So this is your first time?"

He wore athletic shorts, and her hand was precariously close to his dick.

"Yeah, but maybe now's not the right time." He stood.

"Isaach!"

"Oh. Thank you, Miss Paulson."

He got out of her classroom as fast as he could.

Dayum, she's trouble.

She must've been watching him all this time. He hated that. It made him uncomfortable that she'd been so predatory in her own classroom. Thankfully, she was no longer his teacher.

Something was up with that. It didn't come from nowhere. She must have seen something. Maybe she was jealous of Nikki and felt like she had to move in.

It was only eight o'clock. He had forty-five minutes until the bell. He wished DaShon was here to shoot hoops, but he was always late.

"What's going on, Isaach?" Mr. Da'Trin apparently liked to come to work early.

"Doin' okay."

"You're here early."

"Yeah, I was gonna catch a tutoring session."

"Then be on your way, Isaach. It's already eight."

"Yes, sir."

Da'Trin was another one he wasn't sure about. He was friendly and seemed to understand teenagers. But the security guard always pried into everyone's business.

Isaach could go up to Nikki's classroom, but that would be like student suicide. He had to keep away from her at school, as much as he hated that. But it was the only way to protect her position here.

I shouldn't have gone to Paulson's room.

She could turn the situation around and say something had happened. He needed to be on his guard. Life at Grayson High became stickier by the day.

He made his way to the cafeteria and had a seat. This would be a good place to mind his business and be around other students. Those who received free or reduced meals arrived early for breakfast. Isaach always ate at home but sometimes hung out with DaShon when he showed up on time.

Siera sauntered along the cafeteria wall, looking right at him.

Great.

Fortunately, Mr. Da'Trin, who always seemed to turn up like a worm after a good rain, had just come in.

Isaach got up and walked over to Da'Trin before Siera could get too close.

"Everything all right, Isaach?"

"It's good."

"No tutoring?"

"No, not today."

Da'Trin gave him an odd look. Isaach lingered, trying to come up with something else to say.

"Oh. So why you here so early then?" Da'Trin's brow furrowed.

"Thought I needed some help, but I'm good."

Da'Trin nodded. "Take a walk?"

"Sure." Isaach walked with him out of the cafeteria.

"Anxious for basketball practice to start?"

"Yeah. Coach Williams should be having tryouts soon."

"How do you feel? I mean, it being your last year here."

Isaach clapped his hands together. "Anxious to move on."

They stepped outside. Mr. Da'Trin spoke in a low tone. "So what's really going on with Siera?"

Pressure boiled in Isaach's head.

This nigga's got nothing better to do than harass me about Siera?

"I guess she's just trippin'." He pulled his phone out and showed Da'Trin the text. "See this? Look at the date and time. She sent it after that time you said something to me about her."

Da'Trin looked at the phone. "I see what you mean."

Isaach glanced across the parking lot. Nikki stepped out of her car, lugging a few book bags with her.

"Can I help you with that, miss?" Mr. Da'Trin spoke before Isaach had a chance.

"I'm fine, thanks," she said as she approached.

"I got it," Isaach said, and took the bags from her.

"Oh, thank you, Isaach."

As he stepped back into the building, he saw a stern look on Da'Trin's face.

Did I just make a big mistake?

The security guard might have picked up on something. Maybe it was because she had accepted help from Isaach and not Da'Trin. Or maybe it was something else.

Is the chemistry that obvious?

They climbed the stairs to the second floor.

"Maybe I shouldn't have done that," he said.

"Why not?"

"You turned down his offer of help. Then like an idiot I just grabbed your bags."

"Oh, I didn't think about that."

"Yeah, Da'Trin looked at me funny."

"He's kinda annoying."

"How so?"

"I mean, he's been nice enough," Nikki said. "But he always seems to have to say something every time he sees me."

"Like what?" Isaach paused on the landing.

"Nothing in particular. He's probably just being friendly."

He frowned. "This isn't exactly a friendly town."

"You noticed that? I thought it was just me because I'm new."

"Naw, people are like that no matter how long you're here. Everyone is in their own clique."

They were alone on the stairs. He wanted to kiss her right there but didn't dare.

**

A heat burned inside Nikki. She shouldn't be alone in the stairway with him. She shouldn't be alone with him anywhere on campus.

"Are you okay?" He was already at the top of the stairs.

"Yeah," she mumbled. She followed him up the stairs, her hand gripping the banister as she ascended toward his fine muscular form.

Get me outta here.

How could she continue to teach like this when one of her students made her swoon?

"Just put them down on the floor, thanks," she said as they reached her classroom. She held the key in her hand but didn't unlock the door. It would be too tempting with her and Isaach alone in the room.

"Have a good day." He smiled. The expression on his fine angular face made her moist. It matched the expression on his face right before they'd made love for the first time.

"Thanks, Isaach. You, too." She turned her back to him and waited for him to walk away. He didn't. The heat filled her belly. She held the key in her moist fingers but did not dare turn the lock.

"I'll see you later." Since her back was turned, his hot breath hit the nape of her neck. He stood so close. Her pulse soared, and that familiar tingling tickled her core.

They were in the hallway and anyone could walk up the stairs. Faint background noises indicated some teachers were already in their rooms. Any one of them could step out into the hallway.

Nikki put the key in the lock and turned the handle.

"I'll take these inside for you." He bent over to reach for the bags.

"No, leave them there."

"It's no problem."

Nikki turned to face him. "Yes, it is a problem. I'd like you to leave them there."

He made eye contact with her and nodded. "See you." He finally retreated toward the stairwell.

Nikki rushed into her room and closed the door. Her head was spinning and she needed the bottled water she'd brought with her. It was outside the classroom in one of those bags.

She opened the door to the hallway and stepped outside.

When she bent over to retrieve the water bottle, Isaach stood in the doorway of the stairwell. She ached for him.

She quickly returned to the classroom, opened the bottle, and drank some water. It did nothing to quell the fire within her.

This is insane.

The classroom door opened. Nikki closed her eyes. The door gently closed, then his arms wrapped around her. She tilted her head up and his lips pressed against hers. The water bottle slipped out of her hand, but she didn't care. She threw her arms around his neck and pushed her tongue out to meet his.

How did this happen? She should push him away and tell him not to come back, but she wanted him. After that time together in his bedroom, there was no turning back. She hungered for more.

She broke away just long enough to catch her breath. "Isaach, you have to leave."

"I know," he said and kissed her again. His big arms wrapped around her and her body temperature intensified as she'd become consumed with heat.

One of his hands grabbed her butt. She was terrified someone would see them, and she wanted to push him away. But his kisses paralyzed her.

His mouth moved to her throat. He licked her neck and whispered in her ear. "I know we gotta be careful."

"This isn't being careful." She could barely get the words out. His tongue on her tender flesh caused a growing heat in her belly and an ache between her legs.

He slipped one of his strong arms around her waist. His other hand reached under her dress and rubbed her moist panties. He pushed them aside and his fingers slipped inside her.

"Isaach!" As soon as his name came out of her mouth, Nikki realized she spoke too loudly. Someone could have heard her.

He placed his lips to hers and silenced her with a deep, wet kiss. His fingers glided in and out of her, and his thumb stroked her clit. Her body quaked and waves of pleasure rumbled through her.

Her breathing labored, she wanted him so badly. Isaach pulled his fingers out of her and placed them in his mouth.

"Isaach, please leave now."

He nodded. "I know, I'm—"

"Don't say it. Just go before someone sees you."

He left the room. She glanced at the floor. Her water bottle had spilled, and she needed to get that mopped up before her first class arrived.

She buzzed the office.

"Office."

"Can you send a custodian up to B-211 for a wet spill?"

"Got it."

She opened the door to retrieve her book bags. Da'Trin stood in the doorway of the stairwell, gazing at her. Nikki momentarily froze and then ducked back into the classroom.

CHAPTER TWELVE

Nikki silently cursed herself for allowing that to happen. She hadn't merely allowed it—she'd wanted it. Fear replaced the pleasure that had permeated her body. Da'Trin must have heard something, or at the very least, have seen Isaach leave her classroom.

The knock on the door startled her. Da'Trin didn't wait for her to answer—he let himself in.

"Everything okay, miss?"

"Fine." She was anything but fine. Her face had to be as pink as a grapefruit.

"You know you left those book bags in the hall."

"Yes."

"That's a safety hazard. Mind if I move them inside for you?"

"Go right ahead."

Da'Trin carried the bags in and put them on a table. "What's wrong, miss?"

"Nothing. I just spilled some water on the floor."

"What was Isaach Madison doing in your room?"

Where was this going? Her pink face had probably turned crimson.

"He carried the bags up for me."

"The bags are out in the hallway. Isaach was in your room."

A jolt of panic raced through her. "I told him to leave them outside."

"Why?"

She looked Da'Trin in the eyes. "I'm sorry if I caused a safety hazard, Mr. Da'Trin. I appreciate your help. Thank you for your concern."

Da'Trin stared at her for a moment. Nikki held his gaze until he nodded and left the room.

She stared at the door long after he'd left. This wasn't good. He had always seemed like the prying type, and now he was surely worse.

She glanced at the clock. Barely eight thirty. This promised to be a long day. The door opened, and she swung around.

"Hello, miss." It was a custodian, wheeling in a cart of cleaning supplies. "You had a wet spill?"

Nikki pointed to the area. "Right over there." *Maurice* was printed on his name badge. "Thank you, Maurice."

"No problem, miss."

She had to get herself together so she could face her first class in fifteen minutes. She reached for her handbag and pulled out a hairbrush.

"You need this, miss?" Maurice held an empty water bottle in his hand.

"Oh, no." She took it from his hand. "I'm sorry, I forgot to pick that up." She tossed it in the trash.

"No problem, miss."

What next?

While Maurice tended to the cleanup, she reviewed her materials for the day.

Maurice approached her desk and tossed something into the trashcan. After he turned his back, she glanced into the bin. It was the cap from her water bottle. Nikki sighed. She was a bundle of nerves and had four long classes to teach.

"All set, miss."

"I appreciate your help."

"No problem, miss. Happy to help." Maurice nodded to her.

She nodded and went back to her lesson plan. This job was tougher than she'd anticipated.

No, I'm the one complicating it.

One of her own students had brought her to orgasm in the classroom. She had to take responsibility for getting involved with him. Isaach had a powerful allure, and Nikki had to learn how to deal with it.

Now. Before it's too late.

The school year had only begun. She could go back to her advisor at Arcadia and ask to be reassigned, but that would be too risky. Besides, she'd waited too long to register for student teaching. Nothing would be available at this point.

Maybe I can get someone to switch with me.

That seemed so unlikely. It wouldn't be in anyone's best

interest to do that. Then again, she could just say the assignment was not a good match.

**

Isaach shot some hoops with extra vigor. He had to release the tension somehow. He knew what he had done with Nikki was wrong but at the same time, so right. He wanted to be with her.

He and DaShon were drenched in sweat.

"You're quiet," DaShon said.

"Need this workout."

Isaach needed another kind of workout but that would have to wait. His dick strained against his athletic shorts, and right now it was best to keep moving. It would be less noticeable that way.

"Madison!" Mr. Da'Trin did not look happy.

Shit. What does he want?

DaShon looked at Isaach.

"Be right back," Isaach said.

He crossed the gymnasium to Da'Trin. "Yes, sir?"

Da'Trin led Isaach just outside the gym doorway.

"What were you doing in Miss Dayton's classroom?"

There he goes again.

His temples pounded. He wasn't in the mood for this. "Nothing."

"Isaach, don't play me."

"You saw me carry her bags up the stairs."

"And?"

Isaach stared at him. He wanted to tell him where he

could go, but Isaach was raised better than that.

Da'Trin frowned. "I want to know what's going on."

"Nothing that relates to your job as security guard."

"You can look down your nose at me with all your family's money, but I don't like your attitude. If there's something going on, I'm gonna find out."

"For what purpose?" Isaach asked.

Da'Trin didn't answer.

"Didn't think so." Isaach turned his back on Da'Trin and headed back into the gym.

As expected, he found DaShon full of questions.

"What's that all about?"

"Nothing."

DaShon nodded. "You been sayin' that a lot lately."

"He's just all up in everyone's business." Isaach picked up the ball and dribbled.

"Somethin's goin' on," DaShon said.

Isaach continued to dribble. Talking about the situation on campus to anyone was potentially dangerous. It was probably best he not say anything. What he and Nikki were doing was not illegal but highly unethical.

"Isaach, it's not like you to get into any trouble."

"I'm not in any trouble."

Am I?

"You're not messin' with anyone you shouldn't, are you?"

Isaach shook his head. It was Nikki who could potentially face consequences. She could lose her position here and jeopardize her degree. The worst that could happen to Isaach was suspension.

DaShon didn't look convinced. Isaach couldn't really hide anything from him because DaShon could read him too easily. It was only first period and this was already a messed up morning.

"You need to pass the twelfth grade."

They were walking to the locker room, and DaShon's words caught Isaach off guard.

"Why'd you say that?"

"I mean, don't mess it up. This is your last year. You gotta pass everything to go on to college." His words rang true. "Isaach, you got, like, scholarships and shit to think about. Don't do anything to mess that up, or mess up gettin' accepted anywhere."

Isaach hadn't realized it was that obvious. Either DaShon knew something was up with him and Nikki or he strongly suspected. Either way, Isaach had to play it cool for her sake.

"I'm gonna be all right." Isaach wanted to be more honest with DaShon, but he had to protect Nikki. He hoped he hadn't disappointed his friend by avoiding the real talk. He knew DaShon really cared and looked out for him.

Today was Thursday. One more day, then fortunately, it would be Labor Day weekend. Isaach still had to survive today and tomorrow.

He could limit his contact with Nikki to Arcadia, but that wouldn't be enough. He was only there one night a week. He would gladly drive out there on the weekend to be with her, but she had a paying job.

How did she do it? She had to be a full-time student teacher by day with no pay and she balanced that with a full-time waitress gig on nights and weekends. Superwoman.

He could invite her to his place after school, but that conflicted with her work schedule most nights. In some ways, her life mirrored DaShon's. He worked full-time and went to school full-time. His goal was to put some of his earnings aside for building a future for himself.

I had everything handed to me.

**

As Nikki drove to work, she reflected upon the big problem she needed to solve—and do it ASAP. Fifth period had been torture. She did her best to stay away from him, but the heat had raged inside her for the seventy-five minutes they were in the room together. The few times their gazes had met, her body had flushed with heat.

The restaurant featured quite a crowd when she arrived. A busy night made the work go by faster. She changed into her uniform and managed to avoid running into Don. She wasn't in the mood for his attention tonight. Not that she ever was.

"Hey." Don stepped out of the men's room, adjusting the belt on his pants.

Spoke too soon.

"Hey." Nikki didn't even look at him as she stepped past him and into the dining area. She needed every tip she could get tonight. Her goal was to sock away as much money as she could to get herself an apartment—and get out of that dorm room. Another step toward independence.

If nothing goes wrong.

Nikki raised an eyebrow when she saw Carla and The Stud seated in her section. Carla never came here, but her boyfriend often ordered takeout.

"What's up?" Nikki smiled.

"Hey, hungry man wanted to come here." Carla grinned at her man. His name was Mark, but Nikki made up a bunch of names for him. Like Fuck Machine. Creepy. Mr. Not-So-Wonderful. He seemed like the controlling type, so Nikki usually didn't pay him any attention.

"What's good today?" Mark asked.

"Don't know, just got here. Let me get you some drinks and find out. What would you like?"

"Two Cokes," Mark said.

"Coming right up." Nikki headed for the kitchen.

Mark the Wonder Penis.

From the way Carla described him, he knew more about sex than Dr. Ruth. Nikki couldn't care less. She noticed how he'd ordered the drinks for both of them. Controlling. Or maybe it was just a man thing.

Isaach is all the man I need.

It was unhealthy for Nikki to be thinking about her student, but he was so much more than that. She was an adult. He was an adult.

And he's a student in my classroom.

She was here to wait on tables, not dream about Isaach Madison. Yet it was so easy to dream about him. Her thoughts drifted to that tall frame, beautifully sculpted physique, and warm smile.

"Earth to Nikki." The manager gave her a look. "That

table is not going to serve itself."

Nikki nodded and kept moving.

This is dangerous.

One more day of Grayson High and then she could enjoy a three-day weekend. Perhaps enjoy wasn't the right word, as she'd be working most of that time. That was a good thing. It would keep her busy. She needed time to sort out her situation at Grayson. Paulson and Da'Trin seemed to be on to her, or at least suspected something. That wasn't good for either her or Isaach.

Nikki served a table of somewhat irate customers who had waited impatiently. She apologized profusely then returned to Carla and Mark.

"What'll it be?"

"Two blue plate specials." Mark handed her the menus.

Nikki put on her best smile. "Coming right up."

What a creep.

Mark was exactly the type of man Nikki avoided. That might be why she was so driven to work hard. She didn't want to depend on a man. Carla seemed to depend on Mark to make decisions for her and to fill her time. Nikki found it curious that he even allowed Carla to live in the dorm.

Planning period.

Nikki could swap it. Maybe. If there was another senior English class third period, perhaps she could take over that class and she could have fifth period for planning.

Mrs. Ramos will ask why.

Nikki had to come up with a compelling reason. It wouldn't be easy, but she would think of something. She had to get out of being in the same room with Isaach for an hour and fifteen minutes each day. That was torture.

When her shift ended, Nikki was tired yet restless. She wouldn't be able to sleep—too much on her mind. Against her better judgment, she stopped at the Campus Grill rather than going to bed.

It was far more crowded at night than during lunchtime. Nikki found a table in the back of the room and grabbed a seat. She wasn't hungry but restless and needed a diversion.

The act on stage was someone she'd never heard before: Syx Synce. He was a young artist from Houston, slim, tattoos covering each arm. His performance was a revelation. He represented everything a good artist should possess. From the way he moved on stage, his presence elevated the venue. The energy in the crowd was so high that the small campus dive seemed like an arena.

Syx wore a simple crucifix around his neck, the gold framed by his bright scarlet shirt. He moved across the stage like he owned the place and owned the audience.

Nikki bought his CD as soon as he walked off the stage. The act that followed was abysmal. No one could follow what she'd just seen. A young artist destined for success.

Nikki enjoyed music as a hobby, and wished she had more time for it. There was never any money when she was a child to pursue any kind of lessons. But music class was her favorite when she was in school, and she loved playing with the instruments that were available to her in the classroom. The tambourine had been the one she liked most.

One thing for certain, when she returned to her dorm

and turned the key in the lock, Carla wouldn't be there. She was sleeping with Mark the Fuck Machine.

Nikki tossed the CD on her desk, still pumped from seeing such an amazing talent. She doubted she could sleep with her adrenaline spiked. The artist had passion. He had command of that house, and energy had filled the air.

Nikki had found her own passion. She wanted to teach, and she was following her dream.

If I don't fuck it up.

Isaach had to find his. He claimed he wanted to succeed in business, but that was vague. He'd never expressed anything specific.

The only thing he had expressed was a desire to be more independent. That was clearly something he needed, and he'd have to work hard to achieve it. He had a shiny new car, a big house, and a good family upbringing. Two successful parents and a maid. He had it made, all right.

Nikki understood his struggle—he'd had it too easy. Something was missing. Emptiness festered inside him. He needed to fill that void, and he needed to do it on his own terms.

She glanced at the clock. It was nearly midnight, and she was thinking about Isaach. She should be hitting her head against the pillow and getting some much needed rest. Tomorrow was Friday, and she still had a full day of work ahead of her. Work plus work, actually, since she was scheduled at the restaurant tomorrow as well.

Her mind was racing. What to do? She didn't drink, but she was twenty-one and kinda wished she did just to help her sleep. No, that wasn't smart. She didn't depend on anything. She sure as hell was not going to depend on a glass of wine.

I need Issach.

The man unleashed a passion in Nikki that had been dormant too long. She needed to find balance in her life besides working hard. That was an understatement—she worked her ass off. She needed to find some outlet, something to look forward to beyond the hours of labor.

Isaach Madison.

Nikki savored that moment in his bedroom when she'd parted her legs and allowed him to enter her. His energy and his power had plundered into her and she wanted more. She wanted Isaach Madison in her life.

But she couldn't let her relationship with Isaach fuck up her career. She was in her fourth year of college and needed this student teaching gig to earn her degree.

I can't sleep.

She had to face one more day before the three-day weekend, but her mind would not rest. Too many thoughts cluttered her mind, rendering sleep impossible.

**

The next morning, she dragged herself out of bed. As expected, sleep had been fitful. She'd tossed and turned all night. This promised to be a long day.

During the drive to Portsmith, Nikki reflected on her fifth period class and how she had to get out of it. She tried to come up with a reason to present to Mrs. Ramos.

Unfortunately, she couldn't think of anything. Asking to change her schedule would be harder than she'd thought.

When she arrived on campus, Mrs. Ramos wasn't in her office. That was probably best for now. Grayson was a large school. There must be someone she could swap with. It would be helpful if Nikki could find out that information before meeting with Ramos.

She went into the ladies' room and ran a brush through her red hair. Tired, she needed to get to the end of this day.

A day that hasn't even begun yet.

CHAPTER THIRTEEN

Isaach took a deep breath and stood in the doorway of his counselor's office.

"Good morning, Miss Anders." His voice soft, he was a bit embarrassed to be asking her for help.

She looked up from her muffin and coffee with that *what now?* look on her face.

"Can you help me with something?"

"What is it?"

"Job applications." Isaach shifted from one foot to the other.

Her expression was deadpan. "They're all done online. What do you need help with?"

"I've never filled one out before."

Her eyes narrowed. Didn't she believe him?

"I just need some help getting started."

Miss Anders put down her coffee cup. "Isaach, what's this really all about?"

"Ma'am?"

"Anyone can show you how to do it. You're smart

enough to figure it out yourself. What's going on?"

"I just don't want to mess up." He shifted in his chair. Maybe she wasn't the right person to ask. He must look ridiculous. A nineteen-year-old man who hadn't applied for a job before, and he was asking his high school guidance counselor. Other kids probably just went out and did it on their own.

"Isaach, what's really going on here? I sense this is about more than just applying for jobs."

He didn't particularly care for Miss Anders's blunt demeanor. She wasn't someone he would normally trust. "I'm just trying to establish some independence."

Anders nodded. "Nothing wrong with that. I would say it's about time."

Isaach bristled. He had more than his share of people who had an attitude toward his family. The town's population ran from poverty to wealth, and his parents, both being doctors, stood at the high end of the spectrum.

"Where should I begin?"

Anders finished her coffee. "Depends on what you want to do." She picked a piece of muffin from her teeth.

"Not sure."

"You need to start somewhere. Do you want to work indoors or outdoors?"

"Doesn't matter."

"Actually, it does. If you're sensitive to temperature changes, you certainly don't want to work outdoors in Louisiana. You'd be coming to work with winter clothes in the morning and be stripped down to your shorts by afternoon."

He didn't see the humor in her statement. "Indoors."

"Good. What are your skills?"

"I'm good at math."

"That's a good start. Math skills are beneficial in many careers, but it sounds like you just want a part time job you can do around your school hours. Correct?"

"Correct. For now."

"There aren't all that many part time jobs that require math skills. Perhaps a cashier at a store."

"Yeah, that sounds good."

"That's really what you need help with, Isaach. Identifying your skills and then deciding what type of job to apply for based on those skills."

He nodded. At least she was trying to be helpful.

"You don't need any help filling out an application online. You're smart enough to do that on your own."

"I get it now."

"So you're good at math. Go apply for jobs that involve math."

"Cashier."

"That's a good place to start. Or a waiter. Restaurants are always hiring. Laundry centers. Convenience stores. Places that deal in cash transactions."

"Okay, will do."

"Let me know when you get something."

He didn't believe she had any genuine interest. It was more of a dismissive statement.

As he headed to boys' athletics, he still had to come up with a solution to fifth period. He needed the credit to graduate, and Anders wouldn't let him change classes.

It was too dangerous to be in the room with Nikki.

But he wanted to *really* be with her. It was true that he had many young ladies on campus after him. When he'd first become sexually active a few years ago he was like a kid in a candy store. Since he'd met Nikki, he'd lost interest in seeing anyone else.

The question he struggled with was that of fidelity. He didn't have such a good track record with that. But she wasn't like other women he dated. Fiercely independent and strong, she worked hard for her money and everything it bought her.

He thought about her all the time. Was she the one?

She's still my English teacher.

He wanted to hold her and feel her by his side. Cup her sweet, beautiful face in his hands and kiss her. She had a fire within her that hadn't reached its potential. Nikki took it to the next level. She was someone who went beyond what he'd had with young women so far.

Focused and driven, she needed a strong, stable man. He wanted to be that man.

He had a three-day weekend coming up, and he had to see Nikki. She'd likely be working, but he was determined to see her around her work schedule.

Isaach entered the gym and looked around for DaShon but didn't spot him.

He could be out today.

Maybe shooting some hoops would take his mind off of Nikki. His big bone was already pressing against his underwear.

Later that afternoon, when the fifth period bell rang, Isaach ascended the stairs to the second floor of Grayson High School's B Wing.

When he entered the classroom, several students were there, and Nikki stood by her desk tapping on her iPad. On the board were instructions to begin an assignment. He took his usual seat in the back of the classroom and tried to focus.

Nikki looked radiant in a white dress and red shoes. She dressed far better than most of the younger women he knew, which was a testament to her professionalism. Her style also made her hot as hell.

She hadn't yet acknowledged him. Probably best she didn't. The rest of the class filed in, noisy as always, and took way too much time to settle into their seats. Nikki seemed preoccupied with something at her desk and barely glanced at the class. She pointed to the board.

"Your assignment is up here. You have to log on to the school account. It's a timed assessment so as soon as you hit start, you have sixty minutes. It will not take any of you that long, I promise."

Isaach's dick swelled. He held his iPad over his crotch and signed in.

**

The heat spiked throughout her body as soon as he walked in the room. The warmth in her belly, the tingling sensation between her legs, and the dampness inside her all revealed his presence.

Isaach Madison was solid man. It was impossible for her

not to be aware of him and for her body to not respond accordingly. His smoldering sensuality drew her to him.

But it was so much more than that. His kindness. All he'd done for her. The vulnerability he'd revealed to her. Far more than sex drew her to him.

She'd come up with an assignment for today to keep the students' eyes on their iPads and not on her. Isaach would hopefully focus on his work. She would have to do everything in her power to stay away from his side of the room.

He's like a magnet.

The air conditioner defaulted at seventy degrees and could not be turned any lower. Moisture gathered at Nikki's hairline. She reached for a tissue and blotted her brow. A hot Friday afternoon in Louisiana only got hotter.

"Keep your eyes on your own work," Nikki said.

It was a reminder they didn't need. They were a good group of kids. No, they were a good group of young adults. Nikki had to remain alert and focus on the class for the rest of the period. What Isaach had awakened inside her made her about to swoon.

How can I trust what I feel?

He was a nineteen-year-old basketball player, handsome as hell, who probably had every girl in this high school lined up to be with him. He had a sexy car, a sexy swagger, and came from a successful family. Nikki came from poor white trash and had clawed her way out of the garbage heap to get somewhere.

Where am I?

She had worked multiple jobs to live independently. She was in her last year at Arcadia and expected to get her degree in May. Nothing would stop her from achieving this milestone in her life.

Isaach glanced up from his iPad and their gazes met. Nikki tried to look away but couldn't. She was looking into the eyes of a man who'd made love to her as her body had shuddered and quaked like never before.

The studs in his ears caught the light and the sparkle distracted her from her thoughts. She glanced away. She wanted him more than she could admit. He set her whole body on fire with his touch and brought her wave after wave of pleasure.

"Miss Dayton?"

"Yes?" Nikki could barely get the word out.

"What do we do when we're done?"

Nikki gestured to the board.

"The early finisher assignment is up there. You do that one on paper."

The kid nodded.

Nikki took a seat at her desk and angled herself so she would not be facing Isaach's direction. She had to see Mrs. Ramos and get out of this class. Her panties were so wet she feared staining her chair.

Had any of the other girls in the class recognized her flushed face? Certainly some of them were sexually active and had experienced what she had.

Perhaps some with Isaach.

Nikki reprimanded herself for her foolish thinking. The

connection she had with him went beyond something random. Yet she ached for him to be inside her again.

Still forty-five minutes of class time. They'd all be finished soon, and she had to come up with something more. The early finisher activity wasn't long enough to engage them for the remainder of class.

This was one of the things a college professor always warned her about at Arcadia. A teacher must always over-plan. That way backup work would be in place. Nikki hadn't adopted that practice.

Her phone buzzed, and she reached for her handbag and pulled out her phone. The text read, *I need to see you this weekend.*

Isaach was smart enough not to do that. How dangerous it could be for both of them. Yet he did it anyway.

Why is he texting me in class?

She dropped the phone back into her handbag and avoided any eye contact with him. On the opposite side of the room, she pretended to take an interest in one of her students' work. The page was a blur. She couldn't stop thinking about Isaach and the heat burning between her legs.

"Miss Dayton, can you check my work?"

It was Isaach's voice, but she ignored him.

What the hell is he doing?

He should be avoiding her as much as she was avoiding him.

"Miss Dayton."

Damn him!

EXPLICIT INSTRUCTION

Nikki glanced in his direction. Isaach's gold grill glistened when he smiled. His face lit up and he looked beautiful, despite that devilish look in his eyes.

She nodded and held up one finger, even though she had no intention of going to that side of the room. She had to put him off so he wouldn't call her name again.

He's calling attention to us.

The tension in the room had to be noticeable to everyone. Nikki glanced around and fortunately most of the students were on task. Perhaps it was only in her imagination, but she feared everyone could pick up on the chemistry between Isaach and her.

Nikki couldn't help it. She slowly gravitated to Isaach's side of the room, stopping at each desk to check what each student was doing. That way, it wouldn't be so obvious that she was moving toward him.

Her heart palpitated. Today was Friday and she had three days to come up with something to tell Miss Bailey. She needed to get reassigned elsewhere.

She approached Isaach's desk. She glanced at his work but was drawn to the tent between his legs. Good thing he sat in the back row. She sniffed his masculine scent and wanted to be with him.

"Good work," she muttered without making eye contact and quickly moved to the next desk.

"Thank you, Miss Dayton." Isaach's bass voice sounded even deeper.

Nikki braced herself against the next student's desk in case she buckled at the knees. "How are you doing?"

157

"Fine, ma'am."

Nikki continued down the aisle and didn't dare turn around. The fire that raged inside her would only intensify if she made eye contact with Isaach again.

Relieved when the school day finally came to an end, she still had to go to her paying job. Fine, it would take her mind off everything else.

Off Isaach.

When Nikki pulled into the parking lot, it was difficult to find a spot. The restaurant had a full Friday night crowd.

Inside, Don had the dishwasher loaded full, which meant the place was doing a good turnaround.

She needed all the tips she could get. Her financial aid had dried up this year and she had to pay the balance of her expenses. Fortunately, Arcadia was a state school and the tuition was not outrageous.

Her phone made the telltale sign of an incoming text message. She wasn't supposed to use it at work but stole a glance at it when she had a chance. *What time u get off work?* She quickly texted back, *Ten.* Isaach's responded, *See u on campus.*

That meant he planned to drive to Arcadia. Better here than at Grayson High. She wanted to see him although it was still potentially dangerous. She wavered back and forth. Conflict of interest? Or interest of the heart?

When Nikki arrived home after her shift, she craved a shower. Isaach was probably on the way, if not on campus already. She hadn't answered his text, but she didn't have to. He'd made up his mind to come this way.

After peeling off her clothes, she stepped under the hot water. The heat soothed her sore neck. Nothing felt better after a shift at the restaurant than a hot shower.

Well, she thought of one thing that felt better.

Isaach.

She checked her phone after she stepped out of the shower, and his text read, *I'm here.* Nikki's heart leapt. No turning back now. She'd see him.

She dressed and went downstairs to meet him.

Isaach stood in the lobby and greeted her with a brilliant smile. His tall frame and handsome face were a welcome sight after a long day. He took her in his arms and gave her a hug.

"How was work?"

"Busy night, but good."

"You wanna take a walk?"

"I do, but I'm tired. Maybe walk as far as one of those benches outside."

Isaach took her hand and led her outside. His touch sent a ripple through her. How could one guy have that effect on her?

They sat on one of the benches outside in the warm night air.

"I'm glad you came tonight."

"I wanted to see you."

"Isaach, I'm probably going to have to transfer out of that fifth period class."

"I know. I already tried. My counselor wouldn't let me."

"So we're on the same page."

Isaach nodded.

At least his head was in the right place.

"Yeah, I know it's tough. I just wanna get up and hold you and I know it's only a matter of time before some of the other kids pick up on it."

"They probably already have. The chemistry is pretty intense."

Isaach squeezed her hand. "What are you going to do?"

"I need to talk to Mrs. Ramos, but I have to come up with a good reason."

"Yeah, I know what you mean. That's why I struck out with the counselor. I didn't have a reason. Well, not one that I could tell her."

Isaach placed his arm around her shoulders, and she leaned against him. Her eyes closed for a moment and she savored his presence. Up until now, all she'd done was work and go to school. Her independence propelled her forward and made her constantly want to better herself. That meant little free time for a social life. Fending off pimply-faced boys like Don was the norm. She'd had a boyfriend here and there but never experienced anything close to the intensity she had with Isaach.

"Then there's plan B," Nikki muttered.

"What's that?"

"Go to my advisor and ask for a reassignment."

"Away from Grayson?"

"Yeah. It's too dangerous, Isaach."

"We'll still see each other. I'll come here."

"I'd like that." She'd like it far more than she admitted.

The sparks he'd ignited unleashed something deep within her. Never had she felt more like a woman than when with Isaach.

"Is your roommate in?"

"No, she's hardly ever here. She just has an expensive place to hang her clothes."

"Wanna go upstairs?"

"Sure." Nikki's feet ached after being on them all day. She wanted to lie down with Isaach next to her.

As soon as they reached her dorm room, he wrapped his big arms around her. Her face pressed against his chest, the rhythmic beat of his heart against her cheek. He rubbed her arm, then rested his hand against the base of her chin. She lifted her head, and he lowered his face to meet her lips.

The stress of the day melted away as soon as she felt his tongue slide into her mouth. She welcomed it, tasted it, and pushed against it with her own. She gripped his back and held him close to her.

The risk, the danger and the tension disappeared from her mind. She wanted Isaach and had to trust her instincts. The way her entire being reacted to his presence was something too strong to fight. If he could continue to come to here, there wouldn't be any harm seeing him on Arcadia's campus.

He slid his hand down to her ass and squeezed it. She probed his mouth deeper with her tongue. His mouth tasted fresh, of a minty toothpaste and a mild mouthwash.

Nikki nuzzled her face in his neck and inhaled his scent. Freshly showered but not soapy. She closed her eyes and let her nostrils fill with the natural scent of his man musk. She licked his neck and Isaach groaned.

"You found one of my spots."

Nikki ran her tongue along his neck, and he groaned louder. Encouraged, she swirled her tongue around his flesh. His grip on her butt tightened, and his strong hands kneaded her cheeks.

"Do the other side," he growled.

She rolled her tongue along his throat to the other side of his neck, dancing along his velvety skin. That elicited deeper groans from him. He cupped her face in his hands and kissed her. His tongue pushed against hers, and she wanted him.

"Isaach." She said his name as she broke away from the intoxicating rush of his kisses. Fire burned in her core and heat burned her cheeks.

He scooped her up in his arms and laid her down on the bed. When his mouth touched hers, her whole body tingled. She hooked her arms around his neck so she could keep his lips against hers.

He cupped her breast, and his thumb rubbed against her swollen nipple. She squirmed at his touch and wanted to wriggle out of the clothes. She pulled at his shirt.

Isaach pulled his jersey over his head. Nikki marveled at his perfectly sculpted physique. The long, slender torso. The lean, solid muscles. His biceps bulged, and she ran her hand along his smooth, buff chest.

She gazed into his eyes. His chiseled features and caramel complexion stared back at her. The shine from his gold grill matched the sparkle of his studs. He pressed his lips against hers and moved down to her neck. He licked her throat just as she had done to him, and his hand gently unfastened the buttons of her top. Once her blouse was open, his kisses moved down her neck, along her collar, her shoulder, and finally her breast. He sucked on her pebbled nipple.

"Isaach…"

His tongue flicked over her nipple, which only made it swell even further. She ran her hand over his hair, firmly keeping his head in place with his mouth sucking on her breast. The dampness between her legs made her rub her thighs together. He slid his hand under her skirt and found her heat. He tugged her panties aside and pushed two fingers into her.

She let out a low, guttural moan. He pulled her panties down, lifted her skirt, and rubbed his thumb over her nub. Her body writhed, and he put his face between her legs. He probed her folds with his tongue, and she couldn't hold back. Her body quaked with a rush of pleasure as she reached climax.

He didn't stop. He continued to lick and explore her wet channel with his tongue until she gave way to another intense wave of heat running through her body. She tried to catch her breath, but he wanted more.

"Take this off." He tugged at her skirt.

She removed her skirt and whatever else she still had on so she was now completely naked for him. Isaach kicked off his athletic shoes and pulled down his shorts, revealing his massive, hard dick. She took it in her hands and stroked it.

He pulled a condom from the pocket in his shorts and rolled it down his long shaft.

Nikki parted her legs and arched her back. Isaach placed her ankles against his shoulders and slowly inserted his black dick into her pink folds. She grabbed his arms and let out a sharp moan.

Isaach stopped for a moment. She nodded. He eased in farther, and she threw her head back. He paused.

"Don't stop!"

Isaach slid in and out of her with short, slow strokes. Loud moans emanated from deep within her. He thrust it in farther, and she grabbed her ankles, pulling them back. He slid in as far as he could and thrust in her hard. She cried out with each pounding.

Beads of sweat covered his forehead. He pushed in and out of her with intensity unlike any other. The tall basketball player set her body on fire. The heat filled her from head to toe, and her body shook with yet another orgasm.

"Shit, Nikki."

Isaach exploded and let out a loud cry. He fell over her, and she held him close. His back was drenched with sweat, and she was so wet she had probably soaked the sheets. For a moment, he held that position and took deep, short breaths. Then, he rolled on his side and pulled her close to him.

His warm chest against her cheek comforted her. She closed her eyes and savored the moment. He'd made love to her in a way she hadn't experienced, and she wanted to fall asleep with her head resting against his chest.

But he was too tall for her bed and wouldn't be comfortable. But for now, she wanted to curl up in his arms and listen to his heartbeat. The bed smelled of sex, but it wasn't an unpleasant smell. It served as a reminder of the intimacy they'd shared.

But can it last?

CHAPTER FOURTEEN

Nikki wasn't sure how much time had passed. She had closed her eyes and caught a catnap. Isaach's breathing had grown deeper, so he had probably done the same. His chest was still hot, but the sweat had evaporated. She rubbed her face against his chest, causing him to stir.

"You okay?" He kissed her forehead.

"Yeah. So relaxed. You?"

"I feel good."

"Even in this small bed?"

Isaach laughed. "It's not so bad if I pull my knees up."

Nikki closed her eyes again. Their bodies shifted and her lips ended up pressed against his nipple. She licked it, then flicked her tongue around it in a circular motion. He let out a groan that encouraged her to continue.

She tasted his skin and inhaled his musk. Aroused by his masculine scent, she stimulated his nipple. After a few more groans, he carefully rolled her over so she was on her stomach. He rubbed her back and his hand glided along her small, round ass. His finger ran along the line of her crease.

He moved between her legs and kissed her butt cheek. His lips moved along her and both his hands held her soft buns. He parted them slightly and his tongue pushed against her anus. With a sharp intake of breath, she froze.

"What are you doing?"

"Giving you pleasure." His tongue danced around her bud, licking it tenderly. She'd never had a man do that to her before, nor had the thought ever occurred to have it done.

He pressed his tongue into her rose and the saliva from his mouth helped ease it open. His tongue was inside her.

"Isaach!"

"How does it feel?"

"Weird but good."

He continued to probe her soft pucker with his tongue. He darted in and out quickly while firmly gripping her cheeks. She squealed, and he pushed in his tongue as deep as it would go.

More saliva dribbled onto her ass. His tongue slid in and out easier. He spit into his hand and rubbed the head of his dick. He spit again and rubbed it some more, then placed the head against her anus.

"You—"

"Is it okay if we give it a try?" Isaach asked.

"I've never done it before."

"I'll stop if you're uncomfortable."

"Okay." She was hesitant, but hey. Why not?

Before she could say anything further, he slipped the head of his dick into her ass. She cried out.

"Just the head," he told her. "Just the head."

Nikki took a few short breaths. She couldn't believe he was doing this to her, and yet she wanted to surrender to this completely new experience. He moved the head of his cock back and forth without taking it out of her ass. The pain slowly transformed into a pleasure that was unfamiliar to her. He stimulated a spot she hadn't known was so sensitive. She ached for more but was silently grateful he started out gently.

He turned her onto her side and wrapped his arms around her. She couldn't move if she wanted to, and he continued to push the head in and out. Her ass was wet now, and the shaft of his dick slipped in an inch or two.

"Isaach." She grabbed his thigh and began to rock her body in rhythm with his strokes. Her head was spinning as he had taken her to a different place, a place she had never been before.

He groaned and pulled his dick out, and it throbbed against her backside as hot sprays of come coated her.

When Nikki opened her eyes again, she squinted from the daylight. The sun streamed through the window. It faced east and had a red curtain hung over it that bathed the room in a warm glow. She hoped Isaach hadn't gotten a sore back from sleeping while scrunched and curled up in the small bed. A quick glance at the clock indicated she still had plenty of time before her first shift at the restaurant. Hopefully she wouldn't have to work a double today.

Isaach's back swelled and subsided with each deep breath. He slept soundly, and she didn't want to move. The warmth of his body heat could make her stay in bed all day. If only she could.

She rolled onto her back and pulled the covers around her neck. The air conditioner still hummed, and the room was a bit too cool. She nestled up against Isaach and draped an arm around him.

**

Isaach didn't want to leave her. His tall frame wrapped around her and held her close to his chest. The room was fragrant with the smell of sex. With Nikki, he could keep going and going.

I need to stretch.

Sleeping with someone else in a small bed wasn't comfortable. Fortunately he had been tired enough to sleep without moving around too much. But he would pay for it with stiff joints until he did some exercising.

He shifted his body, and Nikki tilted her head up. He kissed her and pushed his tongue deep into her mouth. One arm held her around the shoulders as his other hand rubbed between her legs. He slid his fingers into her wetness and her heat, wanting to be inside her again.

For a moment, he went light-headed. Something about Nikki was different. As soon as he met her, it signaled some kind of change. She wasn't like any woman he'd been with before.

She moaned and probed his tongue with her own. Isaach rubbed her clit with his thumb as his fingers slid in and out of her. He rolled onto his back so she was on top of him. She leaned over the bed, picked up a condom from the floor, and rolled the condom down as far as it would go. With an intake of breath, she eased her channel down onto his long, thick dick.

Holy shit. This white girl was his teacher. And she was riding his cock. A rush of dizziness swam through his head. He wanted her.

"Isaach." Her breathing increased.

Isaach grabbed her hips and gently held her as she guided herself up and down on his morning wood. He stimulated her sweet spot as she rode him, and her face went flush with pink. Her complexion almost matched her hair.

The chemistry between them was dangerous. He wanted to be with her again and again, in and out of bed. There was no turning back.

"Isaach." She called his name loud and clear.

Her movement increased. He rubbed her nub with one hand and grabbed on to her breast with another. She rocked and rode until she cried out his name again and again. Isaach didn't wait for her to slow down. He unleashed his climax and pulled her close to him. He thrust his cock into her as deeply as he could. She let out another sharp moan of pleasure and collapsed on top of him. His dick continued to throb as he released.

They lay still for a long time before he spoke. "What time do you have to be at work?"

Nikki's eyelids slowly opened. She squinted at the digital alarm clock beside her bed. "Soon," she said and closed her eyes, snuggling into him.

"I should let you get ready."

"Hmmmmm."

Nikki didn't move. Isaach eased himself out of the bed and flushed the condom. He did a few squats, amazed he didn't have cramps in his legs from sleeping in such an awkward position. His hamstrings needed to stretch.

"You exercise every day?"

He smiled. "I have to. I'm an athlete."

"I want to see you play."

"Basketball season will be here soon enough."

Nikki slowly dragged herself out of the bed. She looked around the room. "Can you hand me that?"

Isaach picked up the robe she pointed to and passed it to her. She wrapped herself in the robe and disappeared into the bathroom. The sound of water running drowned out any further conversation for now.

He gazed at the ceiling. The morning sunlight reflected from the glass window and onto the ceiling. He watched the light dance as he took a few deep breaths. This was it. His old ways of creeping around were over with. He'd found the woman for him.

Nikki poked her head out of the bathroom. "Oh, there's a coffeepot over there. You want to make some?"

"Do you want some?"

She nodded. He could take it or leave it. He wasn't a big fan of coffee but drank it occasionally. His parents couldn't understand how anyone could be an *occasional* coffee drinker. They drank it every day.

A big jug of bottled water rested on top of the small

fridge, so he didn't have to disturb her in the bathroom to fill the decanter. He got the coffeepot going and was about to do a few more stretches when he noticed a CD on her desk. He popped it into her player. Hip-hop music filled the room.

She likes that?

Later, outside of the dormitory, Isaach kissed Nikki goodbye. A long, lingering kiss for the woman he didn't want to see go. He held her in a strong hug. How could one woman do so much for him? He'd never wanted anyone as much as he desired Nikki.

"I'll see you tonight," he said.

Nikki nodded and got into her car. She waved at him. "See you."

Isaach walked to his BMW. Where could this lead? It seemed so innocent to be with her at Arcadia College yet so dangerous for them to be in the same room at Grayson High School.

He hadn't looked at his phone all morning. There was a text from Siera: *What you doing?* He ignored it. He was hungry, so he texted DaShon, *Meet up at Casey's?* That was a breakfast joint they often ate at. DaShon texted back, *What time?* Isaach figured he'd better go home and take a quick shower, and that was after the forty-five minute drive to Portsmith. *An hour.*

She's incredible.

Isaach hadn't been with someone as giving as Nikki. She wasn't at all demanding of his time, his attention, or anything else. It was refreshing to be with someone like her.

Indirectly, she challenged him to be a better man and become more independent. Most of the women he had been with wanted to drag him down into their own cycle of dependency.

She's independent.

He understood and appreciated that he came from privilege. A family who provided everything he needed. Yet he envied Nikki's resilience. She worked for everything she had and was proud of it. He wanted to feel that sense of pride.

She's insatiable.

Actually, he was the one who was insatiable. She just kept up with him. She had a hunger for intimacy, as though it had been something lacking in her life. Most women were tired out as soon as they were satisfied. Nikki kept him going.

She's my senior English teacher.

As he glided his BMW along Interstate 20, he realized they had to work that out. He couldn't drop the course, because he needed the credit to graduate. He had yet to come up with a compelling reason to tell his guidance counselor. So, from his end, he was stuck with fifth period English unless he came up with a solution.

But he had a three-day weekend to enjoy her company. He intended on making the most of it. Hopefully, she wanted to see him. She'd seemed surprised when he'd said he'd see her tonight.

As he passed through Ruston, he wondered when it'd be the right time to tell DaShon about Nikki. It was no secret among friends that Isaach was sexually active and dated across the rainbow, but he always avoided controversy. He'd never gotten a girl pregnant or caught anything.

When he reached home, he managed to avoid any prying queries from his parents. They respected his age, which, in a way, made Isaach feel sort of independent. Although he hadn't known what independence really meant.

He showered quickly and changed, then headed out again to Casey's. He pulled into the lot and spotted DaShon through the window. They had a habit of meeting here on Saturday mornings if neither one of them had anything else going on. For Isaach, it started as a way to get out of the house early and get something done with his day.

The aroma of coffee and grilled sausages filtered through his senses as soon as he walked in the door. The usual Saturday morning crowd filled the booths and tables.

"'Sup."

"'Sup."

DaShon had ordered a pot of coffee with two cups. Isaach needed food more than coffee but poured some anyway. He didn't look at the menu because he always ordered the same thing. Scrambled eggs with white toast, butter, and potatoes. His favorite comfort food.

"What you do last night?" DaShon asked.

Isaach had struggled with that during the drive.

Do I tell him?

"Hung out."

"Who with?"

"A girl."

"Anyone I know?"

"No." Isaach told the truth. DaShon wouldn't know Nikki. He had junior English.

"Where did you hang out?"

"Her place."

"She nice?"

Isaach nodded.

"What's her name?" DaShon asked.

"She's not from here. You wouldn't know her."

"So where she from?"

"Arcadia. College girl."

"You went all the way to Arcadia to bone a college girl?"

"I didn't say I was bonin' her—to use your expression."

DaShon laughed. Of course, Isaach was busted. He didn't tell DaShon the whole story. If it got around Centerdale, or to anyone in the Portsmith Independent School District, it could spell major trouble for Nikki.

"But you did." DaShon was still cracking up.

Isaach sat back and nodded because he knew DaShon wouldn't let up until Isaach acknowledged it.

"So, why you don't wanna talk about it?"

"Someone new. We just met, so not sure where it's gonna go yet." Did that answer satisfy him? DaShon could read him only too well and was highly inquisitive, so Isaach was doubtful.

"You could bring her around and introduce her to your friends." DaShon refilled his coffee cup.

"In time," Isaach said. *A long time.* It was the first week in September and early in the school year. If he didn't proceed with caution, someone would find out and cause trouble for them.

"Yeah, right. You hidin' somethin'."

Okay, so much for that.

"Nothing you won't eventually find out about." Isaach looked down into his coffee cup. "So what did you do last night?"

"Went out."

DaShon, being only seventeen, didn't have many options. Isaach had gone to his share of clubs that let in eighteen to twenty-year-olds, but it wasn't really his scene. DaShon went anywhere he could pick up girls. Isaach had met plenty of women through athletic events.

"You fuckin' a teacher. That's why you asked me about old lady Hallet."

Isaach bristled. He didn't know what to say. How could DaShon possibly know? He couldn't, of course. He was speculating.

Fortunately, DaShon changed the subject.

"You know, Siera's been sniffin' around, asking about you."

Isaach shrugged. "So?"

He hadn't meant to sound cavalier. He cared about Siera as a person. But he also didn't want any trouble. And he knew Siera had the potential to start some.

"She says you don't answer her texts."

"I don't."

"You know how pissed off she can get."

Isaach nodded. "Yeah, well, I've moved on."

"Apparently she hasn't."

"I don't have anything more to say about her."

"Just be careful, Isaach. You know her temper."

The waitress came and took their food orders. The one thing about Casey's that bothered Isaach was the slow service, but the good food made up for the wait.

He mulled over what DaShon had said. His friendship meant a great deal to Isaach, and DaShon was usually right. Perhaps Siera would try to stir up some trouble.

"Hey, do you know any place I can apply?"

"Apply for what?"

"A job."

DaShon looked at him with speculation. "What do you need a job for?"

"I want one."

"Doing what?"

"I don't know, work in a store or something."

DaShon made a face. "Oh, like all those rich kids who get jobs in museums or the Gap because their parents told them it'll build character?" He laughed.

"No," Isaach bristled. "Nothing like that. My parents had nothing to do with this."

"So where did this sudden urge to join the common folk come from?"

"It's just something I want to do."

"Okay." DaShon sat back and looked at Isaach. "Two ways to do it. You can go door to door, but they are just gonna tell you the second way, which is apply online."

"Door to door, huh?"

"Drive around. See if you see any signs that say NOW HIRING or whatever. Or just go in and ask."

By the time Isaach left Casey's, his head spun with indecision. He wanted to, but he didn't want to. He had the incentive, but he didn't. He had the courage, but he faltered.

After breakfast, he pulled up to the strip mall in the center of town. Nineteen and clueless on how to look for a job. He couldn't help but notice the irony. He sat in his three-year-old BMW while going to apply for a minimum wage job. Hopefully, the hiring managers wouldn't notice his vehicle.

Surprisingly, he found a store with a NOW HIRING sign, just as DaShon had alluded to. It was a large retail chain for women's plus size clothing, and it probably wouldn't have been his first choice.

"Can I help you find something?" The saleswoman's hair was swept up and she wore red-framed glasses.

"I saw the sign in the window."

"The kiosk is right over there."

Isaach couldn't be sure if her tone was dismissive or if she had just said it a dozen times already today. The job kiosk stood in a corner of the store. He had a seat on the creaky old chair and stared at the screen. He hit start and the computer slowly brought him to a sign-up screen. Each time he hit next, the computer took a long time to get to the next page.

I'll be here for an hour.

It took nearly fifteen minutes for him to get through each page. The application included a ridiculous personality assessment. He couldn't believe how much time it took just to apply.

What next?

He needed to get out of here and move on to the next place. From the look on the saleswoman's face, he doubted his phone would be ringing anytime soon. He thanked her on the way out, then stood before his BMW.

It made sense to check out some other stores in the strip mall, so he proceeded on foot. He got the same treatment at most places, but at least he got experience in how to fill out applications.

This is harder than I thought.

Would this ever get anywhere? At nineteen, he still lived at home with his parents. He depended on them for everything and had to break that cycle.

Isaach stood up from a kiosk in a discount outlet store when he spotted Siera. Worse, she spotted him.

She marched right up to him, looked him in the eye, and said, "I think I'm pregnant."

Isaach stared her down. His temples began to throb and his brow moistened.

"What you mean you *think* you're pregnant? Either you are or you aren't."

Siera gave it right back to him. "You know, it's past that time."

"You take a pregnancy test?"

"No."

"Do it. Don't come at me with this *think* shit."

Isaach bounded out of the store. He had always used

protection, so he was confident that she merely tried to get some kind of reaction out of him. Nevertheless, he hoped she'd take his advice, for her sake.

Of course, DaShon was right. Siera would do anything to stir up some trouble. Isaach planned on making sure she took that pregnancy test if he had to give it to her himself.

He needed to go home and chill. He headed back to his car and thought about a well-deserved nap. His muscles were still a little sore from the way he'd slept last night and he wanted to stretch out in his own bed.

He arrived home and walked up the grand staircase to his bedroom. He couldn't detect any sound or movement in the house. Everyone must have been out doing Saturday errands. Dad was probably working. Even Stella might be out or sleeping in. Isaach crawled into bed. Siera's words haunted him.

What if she is?

CHAPTER FIFTEEN

Nikki stood on her feet serving plates of baked chicken with mashed potatoes and carrots. She did her best to get through her shift, although a slightly annoying problem made it troublesome. The throbbing in her anus continually reminded her of Isaach.

He's a freak.

Actually, she didn't really think of him as a freak. He'd just opened her up to new experiences. Her nipples stretched against the fabric of her bra as she thought of him inside her.

Maybe I'm the freak.

"Table five up!"

She had to stop thinking about him, but she couldn't. He had permeated her thoughts, her entire being. He lit a fire in her that nothing could douse. Escalated her to new heights, and there was no turning back.

She grabbed the tray of food and delivered it to table five.

Dammit.

Her panties were wet. She was going to see him tonight.

Her belly surged with warmth as she anticipated what would happen later.

"Can I get a refill?"

"Yes, of course. I'll get it for you right away."

She had had experiences with men before. Correction, with boys. Isaach was all man compared to anyone she'd been with previously. His nineteen-year-old body unleashed an unbridled passion within her. He made her understand the difference between having sex and making love. No man had done that before.

"Hey, Nikki." Don's pimply face was a sight.

"Hey." She wasn't about to encourage any communication with him.

"What are you doing later?"

"I have plans, Don."

She almost pitied him. Nothing seemed to get through to Don that she wasn't interested in him.

After her table cleared, she grabbed the tip and stuffed it into her apron. This promised to be a long shift. At least she had something to look forward to later.

"Nikki, are you okay?" Her boss hovered near her.

"Yes, I'm fine."

"You seem a little distracted tonight."

"I'm fine." Nikki didn't think her daydreaming was obvious.

"Can you work a double tonight?"

"I'm sorry, I can't. I have plans."

"That's not like you to turn down a shift."

He was right. Nikki never turned down an opportunity

to make more money. And here she was, turning down more money for a man. That most definitely was not like her.

"I know, right?"

"Can you work a double on Monday?"

"Sure, no problem."

Monday was Labor Day and it would be busy. She hurried back to her tables and hoped her boss would understand. As driven as she was, she couldn't always work a double. She needed balance in her life.

The text from Isaach came shortly before her shift ended. *OMW.* That gave Nikki enough time to drive home and shower. Her body hadn't recovered from the intensity of his sex last night, yet she craved more.

The night air fanned her face as she drove home. The humid summer heat mirrored the heat generated by Isaach's passion in bed. Nikki feared the seat of her car would stain from the moisture building between her legs.

**

As Isaach cruised along Interstate 20, the encounter with Siera crept into his mind. He didn't believe she could be pregnant, but it wasn't impossible. Stranger things had happened. If it was true, Siera would find some way to make his life miserable. She could go to his parents, although he doubted they would believe her. They weren't particularly impressed with her—or any of his women, for that matter. To be fair, they never were around enough to get to know any of the women he'd dated.

Isaach drove into the parking lot of Nikki's dorm. His

dick was already hard. He had been looking forward to seeing her all day.

When she opened the door, she stood before him wrapped in a bath sheet. Isaach entered and quickly closed the door behind him. He took her into his arms and smelled her freshly bathed scent.

"Isaach," she whispered.

He ran his tongue over her throat and licked her ear. Aroused by her soft moans, he'd been filled with thoughts all day long about how intense they were in bed last night. He wanted it to happen again.

For tonight, he didn't want to think about the conflict that threatened to tear them apart. He pressed his lips against hers and tasted her freshness. The sweetness of her breath coated his tongue. He pulled at her bath sheet, and it fell to the floor. He ran his hands up and down her soft flesh.

"Damn, Nikki."

He crushed his lips against hers, and his tongue danced around her mouth. With her fully naked body against his, he knew he had to get out of his clothes. His dick couldn't be restrained any longer. He slipped out of his shorts and it shot straight out.

Nikki gazed at his cock.

He sat back on her bed and removed his shirt. She knelt before him and took his swollen shaft in her hand. She stroked it with a soft, gentle movement. He put a hand against her full head of red hair and eased her forward. She took him into her mouth.

"Oh, shit!"

He'd messed around with white girls before, but never one who gave him chills like Nikki. A jolt surged through his body when she put her mouth on him. Her wet lips slid an inch or two farther down his shaft, and he groaned.

"Nikki…"

He wore only a gold chain around his neck and his athletic shoes; otherwise he was nude. Nikki got his dick wet with her mouth and made him rock hard. He leaned back on his forearms and closed his eyes. The pleasure overtook him and his mind went wild.

My teacher is sucking me off.

The insanity of the situation could kill the moment. The basketball scholarship hinged on him completing high school successfully. Nikki's bachelor's degree would only be awarded if she completed her student teaching. All of that was at risk.

The pleasure took over and those thoughts were lost to the stimulation of his hard cock. The nerve endings sparked and he felt close to release. He didn't want to come this way, but she sucked his dick like she wanted it.

Her soft white hand stroked his big black shaft up and down. The saliva from her mouth coated his cock and her fingers glided up and down with care. Most girls tugged or yanked at his junk like they were trying to pull it off. Her soft caresses nearly took him over the edge.

She's gonna make me bust.

As though reading his mind, Nikki gazed at him. She sat on his thighs and wrapped her arms around his neck. His hard dick pressed against her belly when she leaned in to kiss him.

Her tongue explored his mouth, and she gyrated her hips against him, whimpering. Isaach could feel her heat when she rubbed further against his shaft. He couldn't hold back much longer.

"Hold up."

He cupped his arm around her waist so she wouldn't fall as he bent over and reached for the foil packet in his shorts, which were crumpled on the floor. She took it out of his hand and ripped it open. She slid the condom over his dick and guided it inside her.

"Isaach!"

She slid up and down on his shaft and grabbed his shoulders. Slowly rising up and down, she moaned. He held on to her butt with both hands, but she was controlling the motion. He let her have her ride, fearing he would bust if he tried to move.

"Baby."

Isaach kept one hand on her butt and moved the other between them so he could stimulate her swollen knot. She bucked up and down at his touch and moaned even louder. He rubbed her until she let out another loud cry, this time her whole body shaking. She continued to ride him up and down, and he exploded as he thrust his hips. Her nails dug into his shoulders.

His breath labored. He would do anything for Nikki. Being with her was like no other experience. His heart palpitated in his chest, and he held her close.

**

Nikki bit into her cheeseburger at the Campus Grill. She was famished from barely eating all day. The cold drink soothed her parched throat after the out-of-breath experience of sex with Isaach.

Tonight's performance featured hip-hop artist Jake Chill.

"He's good."

"I've seen a lot of good acts here." He wasn't eating much. With his size, he should have a huge appetite.

"He's really good."

Nikki paid closer attention to the act. Isaach was right. He had a strong stage presence and noticeable charisma. The Grill had been attracting some exciting new artists.

The night air blew through her mane of red hair as they strolled back to the dorm room. He wrapped his arm around her waist, and her body tingled with excitement over what the remainder of the evening would bring.

When they reached her room, she placed the Jake Chill CD in her computer. Isaach's long arms snaked around her waist and his hardness pressed against her lower back. She arched up on her toes so his bulge rubbed against her ass. He pulled her hair aside and kissed her neck, sending jolts of pleasure through her.

"Touch me," she said.

His hand slipped under her skirt and into her dampness. The heat in her belly and the ache between her legs made it difficult for her to stand. His fingers slid in and out of her, and she balanced herself on the balls of her feet. His strong grip held her in place.

"Isaach." His name came out in a deep breath.

His fingers alternated between rubbing her lips and plunging into her folds. The thickness of his dick against her stimulated the nerve endings all over her body. She gyrated her back against him, knowing it would make his cock swell even more. The scent of his musk had reached her nostrils and ignited her desire.

Nikki turned around and crushed her mouth against his. Hot for his taste, she kissed him with wild abandon. She tugged at his shirt and pulled it over his head. His hard, smooth chest already glistened with sweat. She put her lips around his nipple and licked it.

He groaned and held the back of her head. She brushed her hand against his shorts and grabbed his hard wood. Dropping to her knees, she yanked his shorts down and his cock popped out in front of her face. She took him into her mouth and his groans grew louder.

She gazed up at him. "I got something."

She stood and removed a small bottle of liquid lubricant from a drawer. She rubbed some over the full length of his shaft, and then she turned around and lifted her skirt. She took his dick in her hand and backed her anus against it.

"Go slow," she said.

He pressed his swollen head against her pink rose and pushed it in. She cried out from the sharp pain.

"It stings."

"Once you take the head, the rest'll just slide right in." He grabbed her hips and eased out just an inch and pushed back in. She moaned but didn't cry out. He eased out of her again and pushed right back in.

That initial pain transformed into a pleasure she'd never known existed before last night. The stimulation of her sphincter released endorphins that gave her a major head rush. As his shaft slid farther into her, the familiar rumbling shook through her as her body exploded in orgasm.

They awoke the next morning bathed in one another's sweat. The room smelled of sex as Isaach had kept going all night. The soreness that throbbed within Nikki reminded her of his stamina. She rested her head against his chest and draped an arm over his stomach. She wanted to stay there all day but couldn't—she had a shift to pull at the restaurant.

The weekend flew by. Nikki alternated between standing on her feet all day at the restaurant and surrendering to Isaach's incredible lovemaking skills at night. There were no classes Monday at Arcadia College due to it being Labor Day, but she did have the double shift to keep her busy. She had never experienced as much pleasure in her life as she had this weekend with Isaach.

Earning her bachelor's degree meant more to Nikki than a man. She had to stay focused on that major goal. Busting her butt at the restaurant, she needed to earn the money to pay for her final year of credits. That was her priority, not Isaach.

He sets me on fire.

When she finally crawled into bed on Monday night, sleep evaded her. Thoughts of Isaach filled her mind, and while they comforted her, at the same time, they made her restless. She ached for more of him.

Tomorrow was Tuesday and she still hadn't resolved the conflict of being in the same room with him fifth period. It was only September, and they had a full semester to get through.

How will I do it?

CHAPTER SIXTEEN

The morning heat seared as Isaach drove to school with the top down on his BMW. He didn't mind the heat. While everyone else complained about it, he'd gotten used to it. After all, it was nothing compared to the heat generated between Nikki and himself.

What has she heard?

He didn't know if rumors were bouncing all over the school about him and Siera, but he wouldn't doubt it. It wasn't beyond her to plant a seed. She could tell one or two key people she was pregnant—no, *thought* she was pregnant—and it would be all over the school. Nikki would certainly hear about it.

Damn it, that was the last thing he needed. He hated being the subject of gossip and rumors. He didn't want Nikki dragged into this. He had to find out for sure if Siera was bullshitting or not.

When he wandered into the cafeteria, he found DaShon eating breakfast. He pulled up a seat to join him, although he'd already eaten at home.

"'Sup."

"'Sup."

"How was your weekend?"

Before DaShon could answer, Miss Paulson sauntered by their table.

"Isaach, I have some news for you. Miss Moore posted a bunch of local job openings on the bulletin board outside her classroom. Go take a look at it."

Isaach nodded. "Will do."

"When you decide where you want to apply, come let me know and we'll work on the applications together." She squeezed his shoulder and walked away.

DaShon had that what-the-fuck look on his face. Isaach shook his head. "Don't ask."

"I don't have to," DaShon said. "It's obvious."

"So what'd you do this weekend?"

"Not much. Those three days went by fast. Didn't see much of you."

"I was—" Isaach still wasn't sure how much he could reveal. It would be inappropriate to say anything to DaShon since he was a student here. "You know, just doing stuff."

DaShon nodded. "You've got something going on."

"Yeah, maybe." Isaach smirked. He glanced across the cafeteria and spotted Siera, glaring at him. He avoided her prying eyes.

"And not with her," DaShon said, with a slight jerk of his head toward Siera.

"No, most definitely not with her. Hey, you're well connected here. I need your help with something. Siera's playin' this 'I think I'm pregnant' shit with me."

"She's not."

"How you know?"

"She was dumb enough to tell me she was gonna say that to you just to get a reaction."

"Damn."

"You really don't wanna talk about what's going on, do you?"

"No," Isaach said. "Not yet."

"It must be serious. You're playing with fire."

Isaach avoided eye contact with DaShon for a moment.

"Yes, it's something I'd rather wait to talk about. It's too soon."

"It has something to do with Paulson, doesn't it?"

"No," Isaach said.

Not only was his situation with Nikki serious, it was controversial. Serious was something new to him. Casual dating had been the norm. He'd never experienced the intensity and the desire he had with her. Every time he saw her, he hungered for her like it was the first time.

**

Nikki hadn't slept well. Too many thoughts made her toss and turn the entire night. She dragged herself into the teachers' lounge to check her mailbox. At first glance, she thought it was empty, until her eye caught something in the rear. She stuck her hand in the box and pulled out an old, dog-eared paperback. The title: *How to Make Love to a Negro Without Getting Tired.*

Nikki froze. She tossed the novel back into the mailbox. Then the thought occurred to her that it was evidence. Someone attempted to intimidate her or, at the very least, foster a hostile work environment. She retrieved the book and stuffed it into her bag.

This changed things. She had planned on speaking to Mrs. Ramos today about having her fifth period class reassigned. Now, it was apparent she needed to speak with her about an entirely different matter.

Her mind was spinning. She needed advice but was unsure whom to ask. She didn't know anyone at Grayson well enough. The only recourse she could think of was to call Miss Bailey at Arcadia. Hopefully, she could offer advice on how to proceed. Someone knew about her relationship with Isaach and made a mockery of it.

But if I say something, I'll have to explain.

She had been targeted. If she said nothing, it could get worse. If she said something, her relationship with Isaach would come to light and she'd be fired. Well, not fired. Dismissed.

Nikki pulled her mobile phone out of her handbag. She had Miss Bailey's number saved. Uncertainty plagued her. Her bachelor's degree depended on this gig. One phone call could change all of that.

I don't know what to do.

She could make a what-if call, but Bailey would see right through it. A chill ran through her. This kind of creepiness was not what she'd expected being a public school teacher. Someone was after her, and it was someone who knew about her and Isaach. Or it was someone who at least suspected something.

Before she picked up the phone, she had to find the right words. How she worded this to Miss Bailey could have consequences, yet she couldn't just let it go. The book in her mailbox could be construed as a form of harassment.

I need to make this call.

Nikki took a deep breath and hit call. "Miss Bailey, this is Nicole Dayton. I need your advice on something. I'm at Grayson High School, and someone left something in my mailbox that's sexually suggestive." She listened as Miss Bailey instructed her what to do. It was just what Nikki expected—go directly to the principal.

The door to the teachers' lounge opened, and someone Nikki didn't recognize came in to check her mail. She avoided eye contact. She had to follow through with Miss Bailey's advice.

Fortunately, Mrs. Ramos had finished her morning duty and was in her office.

"Sit down, Miss Dayton." She welcomed Nikki with a warm smile. "What can I do for you?" Mrs. Ramos was dressed in corporate attire, a handsome business suit and silk blouse buttoned at her throat.

Nikki took a seat across from Mrs. Ramos's imposing desk. "I got something in my mailbox. I think someone's intentionally trying to make me uncomfortable."

"What is it?"

"A book." She didn't reach for her handbag.

"And? What made you uncomfortable about it?"

"The title."

Mrs. Ramos frowned. "Are you going to make me guess?"

She pulled the book out of her bag and handed it to Ramos.

"I see what you mean. But what makes you think this was for you? Maybe it was just placed in the wrong box."

"It would be inappropriate for anyone, wouldn't it?"

"Yes, maybe, but why you?"

"Ma'am?"

"You're not African American. Something offended you enough to come to me."

Nikki went quiet. This was exactly what she feared would happen. "It's the sexual nature of the title."

Ramos glanced at the book again. "Yes, I can see that." Ramos removed her glasses. "But I can also see just by looking at you that it's not only that. It's personal. What is it?"

"I don't know who put it in my box." Of course, she strongly suspected it was Sarah Paulson.

"That's not what I asked you, Miss Dayton. There's a personal connection between you and this book or this title or else you wouldn't be here. You would have just laughed it off or tossed the book in the trash."

She got up from her seat. "I need to get to my first period class."

"That's okay," Mrs. Ramos said. "We'll take it up later, if necessary." Ramos handed the book back to her.

She'd had no idea Ramos was so tough. But she was an old lady who had probably been doing her job for a very long time. She could read people well and get right to the core of the matter.

Her legs were heavy as she climbed the stairwell to the second floor. She doubted Ramos would follow up on it, but if she did, Nikki had better have a satisfying answer.

Somehow, she managed to make it through her first two periods. They were her most difficult students, but she kept them busy and got through it. When her break finally arrived third period, she needed to get out of that room.

She had no way of proving who'd left her that book. She thought it was Paulson. In fact, she was almost certain of it. But without proof, it would be premature to confront her or even name her.

Should I tell Isaach?

There would no point in that. He didn't need to know, get upset, or worry about her. He had enough on his plate just getting through his final year of high school. Of course, he could be targeted, too, but she doubted it. This was most likely the work of Paulson. She had noticed the exchanges between Isaach and Nikki and was trying to cause some trouble.

But why?

Nikki wasn't sure what Paulson had to gain from it. Nikki had, in a way, usurped her classes, but that was an administrative decision. Nikki wasn't any threat to her position.

Unless what she really wants is Isaach.

The thought hadn't occurred to her before, but Paulson could be vying for his affections. That might explain some of her behavior during the first week of school.

Nikki wandered through Grayson High's maze of hallways until she found the lounge. It was packed with teachers eating lunch. She glanced at her empty mailbox and turned right back around, not wanting to be around that chatty crowd. She stepped back into the hallway.

"How are you, Miss Dayton?"

She didn't even have to turn around. She knew that voice. It was security officer Da'Trin.

"Fine, sir."

Oh, no. Could it be him?

No, a security officer wouldn't do something that stupid. Only a teacher could be so petty as to have left that book in her box.

"You look a little lost."

Nikki wasn't in the mood for his small talk. "No, just tired. It's been a long morning."

"How are you adjusting?" He grabbed at his trousers.

Is he nervous?

"To what?"

"Teaching high school."

"Fine. It's just a bit overwhelming. I've never been in such a large school. The high school I attended was fairly small." Nikki brushed some hair away from her face.

"Which one?"

"Way out in Arcadia."

"That's where you're from?"

"Yes." She wasn't about to encourage him.

Da'Trin seemed to take more of an interest in her. "You drive from there everyday?"

"Yes."

Does he ever stop talking and do his job?

"Wow, that's a long ways. No wonder you're always tired."

Nikki wanted to slug him. "Thanks for the book."

"What book?"

Nikki looked him squarely in the eye. She could see he had no clue what she was talking about. She didn't think so. She just wanted to eliminate him for sure.

"Oh, my bad. I was thinking of something else."

Da'Trin smiled. "If you do need anything, you let me know, you hear?"

"Sure," Nikki said.

"I can carry stuff from your car up those stairs for you."

"Thanks. But this is my planning period, and I need to get some work done. Excuse me."

Nikki really didn't know where to go. The cafeteria was overflowing with kids. She wasn't hungry, although she should have been. The teachers' lounge was too loud and she needed to relax.

Heading outside, she reasoned getting off campus was the best option. She'd pulled a double at work yesterday and never found the time to make a lunch. She needed to eat something, so she headed out to a sandwich shop she passed every day on her commute into town.

As she stood in line, a voice behind her spoke.

"Hey, pretty lady."

She wasn't certain it was meant for her, but she turned around anyway. Standing directly behind her was someone who looked familiar, but she couldn't place him.

"Hello." She turned again to face forward.

"How's the teaching going?"

"Fine," she said. Her back was still to him.

"We've met before."

She turned back to face him. "And?"

"Devon Jackson. I coach football at the high school."

"Oh, right. And teach algebra."

Jackson let out a hearty laugh. "See, you do remember me."

Nikki forced a smile.

"Can I take your order?"

She turned to the counter and placed her order. She took her numbered receipt and had a seat by the window. Best to take her sandwich to go. Otherwise Prince Charming would certainly ask to join her.

Of course, he did just that. She didn't even have time to blink before he came sauntering toward her table.

"Can I join you, pretty lady?"

"It's Miss Dayton to you. And I'm getting mine to go."

"Well, you mind if I have a seat until the order's ready?"

"Go right ahead." His cologne stung her nose. She wondered if the fragrance was called Arrogance. He kept his eyes on her the whole time with a silly forced grin on his face.

"Thanks, Miss Dayton." The words came out as though mocking her.

What an asshole.

Mr. Jackson was completely full of himself. His lingering looks made her uncomfortable. In the short time she'd been at Grayson, Nikki had learned he had a reputation for building up a strong football team. He also had a wandering eye. She glanced down at his wedding band.

"So, how are the students treating you?" Jackson still had that silly grin on his face.

"Fine," Nikki said. She glanced at her order ticket, hoping her number would be called soon.

"Must be kinda tough."

"How so?" Nikki glared at him.

"You being so close in age to them."

Nikki shifted in her seat. "No, that doesn't make any difference." Of course it did. Isaach was merely two years younger than her. Most of the other students were no more than three or four years younger. She checked her ticket number again.

"I just thought it'd be awkward."

Nikki didn't like where Jackson was going with this. She couldn't remember specifically which of her students were on the football team, but there had to be some in one or more of her four classes. If there were any in her fifth period class, they could have picked up on something between her and Isaach.

"It isn't, Mr. Jackson. What's awkward is sitting here with you." Nikki stood up. She moved closer to the counter and waited for her number to be called.

"I'm sorry. I didn't mean to offend you." He had moved right next to her.

Nikki turned her back to him. Unfortunately, looking at her ticket did not make her number get called any faster.

"I just thought you might like some friendly company during lunch."

Nikki had a sarcastic comeback but kept it to herself. Finally, her number was called. Her order sat on a tray since she'd intended to eat in.

"May I have a to-go box please?" She wanted to get away from Mr. Jackson. The clerk handed her a to-go container, and she quickly stuffed her order in it.

Back at Grayson, she found refuge in the library. Usually, eating wasn't allowed here, but the librarian was sympathetic when Nikki asked permission.

"I wouldn't be caught dead in that teachers' lounge. Sit wherever you'd like."

She found a desk with privacy partitions even though the library was practically deserted. The librarian and her assistant were both scarfing down their lunches while talking with food in their mouths, and Nikki didn't need to look at that.

At least she was away from Devon Jackson. He was trying to get familiar with her, but she wasn't certain if he'd heard rumors about her and Isaach or if he was just a creep.

He's a creep.

He probably chased women left and right, all the while flashing his wedding band. He wasn't a bad looking man. There were probably many women who fell for his false charms.

She'd only been up to the library once before when she'd become familiar with the school. For a high school library, it was huge. Rows and rows of neatly stacked shelves, but apparently not many students used this resource. The librarian kept the vast room tidy. It reminded her more of a small college library.

After she finished her smoked turkey and Provolone, she dumped her trash in the bin and wiped off the table with a napkin. The library was quiet, and she took a stroll around the stacks. She was impressed by the library's collection as she wandered from tall row to tall row of books.

"Hey."

Sitting at a carrel in the rear of the library, his head visible over the partition, Isaach smiled and gave her a short wave. Her face burned with heat at the sight of him.

"Hey, why aren't you in class?"

"I am, sort of. Third period civics. The teacher sent me up here to do some research."

"Oh."

"Why aren't you in class?" Isaach grinned.

"Planning period."

Isaach stood up, took a quick glance around, and then took her into his arms.

"Isaach, don't."

"There's no one here."

"Doesn't matter; it's not the place."

Isaach released her from his hug, then took her by the hand and led her to his carrel.

"We can chat for a minute?"

"For a minute. You know we can't socialize here." She leaned back against the carrel.

"How's your day going?"

"Fine," Nikki lied. She wasn't about to tell Isaach about the book. At least, not yet. "Just tired."

"You pull that double yesterday?"

She nodded.

Isaach took both her hands and held them. He sat back in his chair. She wanted so much to touch him, to smell his scent and taste him. But she couldn't. Not here, where they could be exposed. She shouldn't even speak to him unless in the classroom.

"Hey, you teach study skills in our class."

"I do."

"Then it's okay if you talk to me here. You're just helping me apply what I learn in your class to my civics class." He smiled broadly, and she laughed.

"Nice try, Isaach." She held his hands but trembled. What she needed to do was let go and run away. His touch aroused her.

He let go and slid his hands along her thighs. A tingling vibrated through her legs and into her core.

"Shit, Isaach, are you—" Nikki spoke a bit too loudly and glanced around the room. No one was in sight. That didn't make it okay. His large hands were in a dangerous place, touching her. Closer.

"Isaach…" She cried out his name, not realizing there were others who could hear her. She looked to her right and saw a young woman glaring at her.

"Isaach!" It was almost a scream.

He looked to his left. "Siera."

CHAPTER SEVENTEEN

Nikki froze. Isaach said the young lady's name with urgency. Something was up.

"You muthafuckin' asshole!" Siera screamed.

Siera pummeled her fists against Isaach's chest and face in a frenzy of rage. "You muthafuckin' piece of shit! Now I know who you fuckin'." As she hollered, the librarian and a few others gathered around to see what was going on.

Nikki's face turned scarlet. This crazy young woman continued to beat Isaach as the adults just stared. Nikki couldn't stand to see him abused like this any longer.

"Call security," Nikki shouted.

The librarian's assistant ran to a phone. The librarian stood there like a moron and watched the young hussy hit Isaach. Nikki grabbed the bitch by the hair and pulled her off of him.

Siera screamed like a banshee. Nikki knew she could get in trouble but didn't care. She needed to protect Isaach, who took a gentleman's approach and wouldn't lay a hand on the girl but just allowed her to beat on him. The librarian took a step forward but seemed uncertain what to do. Isaach wisely took a step back at this point.

Siera clawed at her, but Nikki did her best to keep her at bay. "Damn white bitch," Siera screamed at the top of her lungs. "Fuckin' white whore. White slut. White piece of shit."

Mr. Da'Trin rushed into the library and pulled Siera apart from Nikki.

"Cocksuckin' muthafuckin' bastard," Siera screeched at Mr. Da'Trin as he carried

her away.

**

As Nikki sat outside the principal's office, her body shook with fear. This was it. Certain her career was over, she lamented the years she'd spent working toward a bachelor's degree she would not see.

What should I say?

The words swirled around in her mind, but she couldn't come up with a coherent story. Some crazy bitch went off on Isaach, and Nikki tried to protect her student. No, that wouldn't work. Ramos would want to know what set off the young woman.

Ramos had Isaach in her office now. There was no telling what he would say. He wore his honesty on his sleeve. The young man was clearly raised well. He had strong, successful yet somewhat absent parents.

I'm from a trailer park.

Gone to college. Worked for every scrap of clothing.

Worked for the car, her tuition, and her food. But she was still white trailer park trash. Anyone with a brain could see through that façade.

My mother's an alcoholic.

Nikki shuddered at the thought. Isaach's parents were both doctors. What in the world was she thinking? He was leaps and bounds ahead of her in social standing. His parents would look at her as a doormat.

Then again, Stella seems nice enough.

Nikki had not met his parents. Perhaps they were fine like him. His upbringing spoke for itself. He was well mannered and had goals to be successful and independent, just as she did.

That girl had made a major scene in the library. Clearly, Isaach knew her, but their relationship wasn't clear. Nikki didn't really care to know. At this point, the girl represented someone who'd brought down the house of cards.

It was well into fourth period now, and Nikki absently wondered who held her class. Someone probably got the inclusion teacher to do it. The students in fourth period were the best. She shifted her weight, tired from sitting on the old bench.

Isaach came out of Ramos's office. Their gazes met for a moment, but Nikki couldn't read his. He smiled, presumably for encouragement, and walked out the door.

"Miss Dayton." Ramos's voice was commanding.

Nikki got up, even though her legs didn't want to. She had that hollow pain in her stomach, dreading what was about to transpire. Three full years of college including summer school had brought her to where she was now. She was in her fourth year of college, doing her student teaching, and all of it was on the line.

"Sit down."

Nikki sank into one of the chairs opposite Ramos's desk. The office walls were adorned with various endorsements, degrees, and awards. Ramos had worked hard to get where she was, similar to Nikki's own work ethic.

"Tell me what happened in the library."

Nikki took a deep breath. "I was having my lunch—"

"In the library? Why not the teachers' lounge?"

"It was loud and crowded in there, and I wanted to be someplace quiet."

"That's what the teachers' lounge is there for. The library is not a place to eat. Continue."

"When I finished eating, I took a walk around the library. I hadn't really become familiar with it yet."

"Then what happened?"

Nikki froze. She knew her career was on the line and would likely be determined by her response.

"I saw Isaach sitting at a desk."

"And?"

"He spoke to me. He told me he was working on some research for his civics class and asked for my help."

"And?"

"That's it."

"Then why was the young lady so upset?"

"I don't know."

Ramos put her head down for a moment and looked at

some of her notes. "Isaach said he had previously dated her, but they were no longer seeing one another. He also said Mr. Da'Trin knew about their relationship, but I haven't spoken to Da'Trin or the girl yet."

In one manner, Nikki was relieved. If Ramos hadn't spoken to Siera yet, there was still a chance of salvaging this situation.

"Prior to your student teaching assignment here, had you ever met Isaach Madison?"

Nikki hesitated. She hadn't thought about that, but it would lend credence to her side if she was honest.

"Yes."

"Under what circumstances?"

"Arcadia College. He takes a class there and that's where we met."

"When was this?"

"Over the summer, before school started."

Ramos looked down at her notes again. "That's basically what Isaach said. I'm not going to speak with Siera until she's calmed down. Something drove her to hysterics, and I'm going to find out what it is. I suspect there's more to this story than you two are telling me."

Nikki didn't know what to say.

"I'm giving you the rest of the day off until I can complete my investigation." Ramos pressed a button on her phone. "Get Da'Trin in here."

Nikki assumed Mrs. Ramos wanted to speak with Mr. Da'Trin next. She was wrong. When Mr. Da'Trin arrived at Mrs. Ramos's office, she instructed him to escort Nikki to her classroom to collect any personal belongings, then walk her to her car.

"If anyone questions you, Miss Dayton, just tell them you're not feeling well and needed to leave."

"Yes, ma'am," Nikki said. That familiar hollow pain in her stomach intensified.

Da'Trin escorted her and Nikki collected her belongings from the classroom. It was still fourth period, and she made an excuse to the inclusion teacher about being ill.

"Don't worry, Miss Dayton, you'll be all right." Da'Trin spoke to her as he walked her across the parking lot.

"You're sure about that?" Nikki didn't feel instilled with confidence at the moment.

"Yeah, it'll all blow over. No one wants any trouble here."

Nikki wasn't so sure. Mrs. Ramos practically accused her and Isaach of hiding something. There would be no telling what Siera would say. Although she didn't know Da'Trin well, her instincts told her he was trustworthy. When Ramos spoke to him, he would probably stick to the facts.

"Get home safely."

"I'll do my best," Nikki said wryly.

Nikki drove home with a heavy heart. She wished she believed Da'Trin, but she just didn't share his optimism. This situation was far from resolved.

When she reached her dorm room, she figured she had enough time for a nap before heading to the restaurant. If only she could clear her mind enough to fall asleep. It had been one hell of a day.

Nikki crawled into bed and pulled the covers over her. It

was hot, but she didn't care. She just wanted her body and mind to shut down for an hour or so.

It was over. Everything. Gone.

She'd have no career. Perhaps get expelled from the college before she could earn her credits to graduate.

And never see Isaach again. Why hadn't she just stayed away from him in the library? Or anywhere at Grayson. She'd allowed herself to be placed in one compromising position after another.

And it would cost her everything.

She squeezed her eyes closed.

**

Isaach sat in his car in the parking lot of Grayson High for what seemed like the longest time. His senior year hadn't started off on such a good note. What would his parents say if they found out?

Or when they found out?

Found out what? What had really happened? Nothing. Siera had gone batshit crazy on him in the school library. That was it. Nothing more. The top guns at the school couldn't take him down for that.

Ramos was hard to read. Isaach had no idea if she believed him or not. His principal wasn't known for being all warm and fuzzy. She was all about compliance. He wasn't certain how well Ramos knew Siera, if at all. Siera could come across as persuasive when she wanted to be. She'd have no problem exaggerating the situation, and painting a picture in Ramos's mind.

And Nikki. She hadn't done anything wrong. She'd walked into the library, and that was that. Isaach ran his hands over the steering wheel, the same way he'd run his hands along Nikki.

Had Siera really seen that? Or just seen him with a white woman? It wouldn't take much to set off Siera.

But damn, he had to graduate this year. So much to look forward to. So much to plan for next year. College. Athletics. Life.

How much damage could this situation cause? He couldn't stay in Nikki's class. Not after this. But then again, once this all blew over, he wasn't so sure Nikki would even have a class.

CHAPTER EIGHTEEN

The phone ringing woke Nikki. She wasn't sure of the time. Her bag was still on the floor where she'd dropped it, so she dragged it toward her.

"Hello?"

"Hey." It was Isaach.

"Isaach, what's gonna happen?"

"I don't know. School just got out, and Siera's still in Ramos's office."

"After all this time? That's not good."

"Probably not."

"Hey, Ramos said you and I told the same story, but I don't think she believed us."

"No, I don't think she believed me either. Are you okay?"

"Yeah, I think so. I was just taking a nap before work."

"I'm sorry. I woke you."

"Doesn't matter. I have to get up and get ready anyway."

"I'm sorry, Nikki. My actions were wrong. I never should have called out to you in the library. I never should have held you. If anything I did causes you to lose—"

"Hey, stop. Don't think about that now."

There was a pause. "Okay, I won't keep you. Just wanted to make sure you were good."

Nikki laughed. "Not sure I feel good. But thank you. It's good to hear your voice."

"You, too. See you later."

She let the phone drop back into her bag. She rolled over on her back and stared at the ceiling. Somehow, she had to muster up the strength to knock out another shift at the restaurant.

It wasn't a good night. From the moment she walked in, the place seemed to be one big mess. She'd never seen it that bad on a Tuesday. Customers were complaining, her boss had a short fuse, and even Don seemed grumpy. When she found a chance to take a break, she did.

Curiously, there was a missed call from Miss Bailey. Her advisor never called her, and she couldn't imagine why she'd call in the evening. Nikki listened to the voice mail, which instructed her to call back no matter how late.

This has to be bad news.

Nikki found Bailey's name in her directory and pressed call.

"Hello."

"Miss Bailey, this is Nikki Dayton."

"Miss Dayton, your assignment at Grayson High School has been terminated."

Nikki's body went numb. She gripped the phone lest she'd drop it.

"Terminated."

"Yes. Once I receive Mrs. Ramos's report, I'll need to pass it along to the campus disciplinary committee."

"Wait. I paid for the credits. I need to finish my student teaching."

"Miss Dayton, I wouldn't count on anything until you go before the board. I'm sorry."

"Yes, ma'am."

Nikki didn't know what to do. She stood outside the back door of the restaurant, her hopes and dreams on the verge of shattering. She had to find another student teaching position, but from what Miss Bailey said, that might not be an option.

The door swung open and Don came outside, a cigarette already dangling from his lip. His hair poked out of the net covering his head, and his apron was stained.

"How's it going?" He cupped his hand around the lighter as he lit it.

Nikki choked on the one word that eked out of her mouth. "Fine." Her eyes brimmed with tears.

"You don't look fine."

Amazed Don would even notice, she turned away from him.

"Something wrong?"

Nikki didn't answer. The tears streamed down her face, and her shoulders trembled. She had to finish her student teaching to get her degree. Now, it all seemed lost. Don placed his arm around her shoulders, which only made her sobs grow louder.

She didn't care that Don was seeing her break down. She

didn't care that his sweaty arm draped her shoulder, and she didn't care that his pimply face nestled precariously close to her. The only thing she cared about was getting her career back on track. She had to see Miss Bailey and fight to continue at Arcadia.

When Don's dry lips scraped against her forehead, Nikki pulled away. "I gotta get back to work."

"We can talk about it, Nikki."

Nikki shook her head and dashed back inside. She was going to be the damn best waitress she could be if she had to. She wasn't going to let anything knock her down. Tomorrow, she would be at Bailey's office first thing in the morning.

Sleep didn't come easy. Nikki tossed and turned all night. She had let down her guard with Isaach in a dangerous place. Fully aware of the risks, she'd continued to communicate with him at Grayson. Actually, she couldn't help it. She was drawn to him in a way that seemed almost like an addiction.

She awoke on Wednesday morning, groggy from her restless night. She had to see Bailey as early as possible. First, a shower and coffee, which would hopefully help her wake up.

She arrived at Bailey's office early. The door was closed and the lights were off. Nikki went to the student lounge to have some coffee and wait. It was the kind of machine where she had to press buttons to get her concoction, which tasted burnt, but it was better than nothing.

This sucks.

It had taken everything she had and more to save up for college. Sure, she'd received grants and scholarships, as well as a student loan, but she was responsible nonetheless.

A couple of students drifted into the lounge, arriving for their first class of the day. Nikki didn't recognize any of them from the education department. The truth was she seldom socialized with her classmates. She was too busy working. Most of them seemed to be coasting through because they believed education was an easy major and they just had to show up to get some credits.

In an ironic way, they were almost right. The lack of professionalism among some of the professors had surprised Nikki. They were lazy. A three-hour class with one instructor was usually dismissed after twenty minutes. He didn't want to work, but he had been on the payroll for years collecting a check. Another pompous old slob pontificated about her doctorate degree but did nothing in the way of teaching. *Read this book by this date for this test* was her idea of instruction, which totally went against the principles of teaching and learning. No discussion or activities to support the text.

If Nikki had learned anything from these two, it was how not to be an effective teacher. It killed her that she wasn't at Grayson today. She had accomplished so much in the short time since school started. At least, she'd thought she had.

What's going to happen?

Thoughts flooded Nikki's mind. Find a new student teaching gig or find a new college to finish her credits. There was always Grambling.

No, I'll fight to stay here.

Too much was at stake. Nikki had no idea what Siera had said to Mrs. Ramos. Whatever it was, it had resulted in Nikki's dismissal. She doubted Miss Bailey knew the details, or she would have said something more specific on the phone last night.

What a day.

As she gazed around the lounge, she recalled that fateful day she'd met Isaach. After he fixed her car, they'd had their first real discussion here in this room.

She finished her dull coffee and went back to Bailey's office. The door was open.

"Good morning, Miss Bailey."

"What can I do for you?"

Nikki walked in and had a seat. "I'd like to know why I was dismissed from Grayson."

A pregnant pause.

"Suspicions of inappropriate behavior. Your principal will file a report with the college and the committee will take it from there."

"Suspicions? They can dismiss me on suspicion alone?"

"Yes. They can do whatever they want, really."

"What about my student teaching? Can't I just find someplace else?"

"That wouldn't be wise, not until you go before the board. Why put yourself through all that?"

"Because I need to move forward with my degree program."

Bailey sighed. "I can see your point. But with this hanging

over your head, I don't think it's a good idea."

"But it's not forbidden. I mean, I can go look for another opportunity, can't I?"

Bailey nodded. "I suppose you could. They're just going to ask a lot of questions. You can look all you want, but don't expect the college to approve you if you have a disciplinary hearing pending."

"But I don't. You said yourself Mrs. Ramos hasn't filed a report."

"Yet."

Nikki slouched in her chair. She could see where this was going. The college was going to totally support Grayson High's *suspicions* until a hearing. In other words, guilty until proven innocent. She needed to get someone on her side.

**

The hot Louisiana sunshine beat down on Isaach and DaShon as they shot hoops during morning athletics. Isaach was on edge. He was worried about Nikki. It tore him up that he might be responsible for any disciplinary action against her. And something was bound to happen. Siera threw a fit and there would be consequences.

"So you ready to talk?" DaShon didn't look at Isaach when he spoke.

"About what?"

DaShon dropped the basketball. "Come on, Isaach, how long you gonna pretend? The whole school's talking about you."

"What they saying?"

"Siera walked in on you in the library with your face buried in some white teacher's pussy."

"Shit!" Isaach looked around. He doubted any of the other guys heard him.

"Real talk."

"That's not true. They're just talkin' shit." Isaach had to come clean. "Can we talk about this after school? Too many people around."

"You don't wanna incriminate yourself?" DaShon smirked. "Listen, bro. Whatever you got goin' on with a teacher, you gotta stop. You got way too much at stake. Like graduation. Diploma. You wanna risk all that over some white pussy?"

Isaach picked up the basketball and dribbled aimlessly. That sinking feeling hit the bottom of his stomach and he wanted to retch. Something was sure to go down now.

Dayum.

He had glanced around the lot for Nikki's car earlier and hadn't seen it. Maybe she was running late. Something didn't feel right.

After athletics, he sent her a text. As the day lingered on, he still hadn't gotten a response. He heard whispers and gossip about her throughout the day, but he ignored them.

By the time fifth period arrived, it became clear the rumors were true. When Isaach saw Miss Paulson in the classroom, he knew it was over for Nikki. She gave him a sly, knowing smile that made him uncomfortable in more ways than one.

What does she know?

"Good to see you, Isaach. It's been a while."

He nodded and retreated to his seat. Odd she spoke to him that way in front of other students, her voice laced with innuendo.

Or am I reading too much into this?

He glanced around the class, looking for someone to convo with to keep occupied. He spotted one of his teammates. Isaach made small talk with him while the rest of the class filed in.

Miss Paulson is staring at me.

He couldn't shake the feeling she was up to no good. He had no idea what she had against him, but it didn't feel right. Something smelled.

Once the class got settled, Paulson clasped her hands together and stood with her butt leaning against a desk. "As you've heard by now, Miss Dayton will not be coming back to Grayson. I'll be holding this class until Mrs. Ramos decides on a replacement."

There were snickers and snorts throughout the room, and Isaach wondered if the joke was on him. Everyone seemed to have heard something. He sensed by some of the stares and side glances that a lot of people knew. His ears burned.

Shit.

Now he had to sit through seventy-five minutes of Miss Paulson every day. He was angry, but angry with himself for getting Nikki in trouble. It was his fault. If he had just practiced self-control, this wouldn't have happened.

"It's good to be back with you again. I've missed this

class." Paulson looked right at Isaach when she spoke. She made the time drag, sauntering around the class, doing a whole lot of nothing. He glanced at the clock, wishing he were anywhere else.

Paulson finally gave them an assignment to do, which kept the class relatively quiet. She kept herself busy at the desk for a while and then made her rounds up and down the aisles. When she reached Isaach's desk, she leaned over and whispered in his ear. "I don't get tired." She slowly moved away from him.

What's that supposed to mean?

CHAPTER NINETEEN

Nikki sat in the attorney's office, waiting for her appointment. Earlier this morning, she'd remembered one of her regular customers was an attorney. She called in a favor and, fortunately, got an appointment the same day.

"Come in, Nikki." Barbara's friendly smile greeted her as she held the office door open.

"Thank you."

"So what can I do for you?" Barbara gestured for Nikki to have a seat.

"I'm in trouble at the college and my career's on the line. I want to find out what rights I have and protect them." Nikki twisted the straps of her handbag. Lawyers made her nervous.

"What happened?"

"I'm enrolled at Arcadia College. Going for my degree in education. I had a student teaching gig at Grayson High School."

"Where's that?" Barbara leaned back in her chair.

"Portsmith Independent School District."

"Portsmith? Why all the way out there?"

Does everyone have to call attention to that?

"I signed up kinda late. Actually, it's in Centerdale, but it's the Portsmith ISD."

"Okay, and what's the problem?"

In other words, get to the point.

"I got a phone call from my advisor at the college late last night. She told me I'd been terminated at Grayson."

"Terminated. You don't get paid for student teaching, right?"

"No."

"So why did they let you go?"

"According to my advisor, it was suspicions of inappropriate conduct or something like that. Can someone be let go just on suspicion?"

"Where children are involved, yes." She folded her arms across her ample bosom.

"It wasn't with a child; it was an adult."

"So something did happen?"

"Kinda. Sorta. The problem is, I can't finish my degree unless I complete my student teaching."

Barbara nodded. "True. You're going for your bachelor's, right?"

"Yes."

"It doesn't sound like your problem's with the college. Can't you just get another student teaching gig somewhere else?"

"The college said that's not a good idea. Apparently the high school is going to forward some report to the college, and it'll go to a discipline board."

Barbara took a deep breath. "Has the report been sent yet?"

"Not that I know of."

"Good. Start with the high school and see if you can soften the blow. Portsmith is kinda far. I know someone who works for the teachers union here. Let me see if I can find out who to contact in Portsmith."

"I'm not a member."

"Probably won't matter if you're a student teacher. You can't be a member if you're not getting paid, so they might help you." Barbara picked up her phone and dialed a number. "Jen, it's Barb. Who's that lady in Portsmith who heads the union? I've seen her on TV, but I can't remember her name." Barbara picked up a pen. "Yeah, got it. You have a number?" She scribbled something down. "Thanks."

"Wow, that was fast."

Barbara handed Nikki a slip of paper. "Florence Dunn. North Louisiana Teachers' Union. Call her."

"Thanks. What do I owe you?"

"Nothing. Consultation's on me. Just slip me an extra drink next time I hit the diner."

Nikki laughed. It felt good to laugh for the first time since this nightmare had begun.

When she returned to her car, she still debated whether or not to call Isaach. She had received his text earlier, but she'd had too much on her mind. She wanted to be able to tell him something positive. She was too embarrassed now and didn't want him to feel bad over what had happened.

Or did he hate her? This jeopardized his position, too. His scholarship. College applications. It had become too complicated.

And this had been a long day. She needed food, and she needed to call this Dunn woman before she headed to the restaurant.

Much to her relief, Nikki got an appointment for the next morning at eleven. Once home, she hopped in the shower and got ready for work. She needed all the strength she could muster to make it through another shift with so much on her mind.

How can I face Isaach now?

There was no telling what the school had done to him. He was in his senior year, poised to graduate, and now this. A star athlete on the basketball team, an advanced student, being dragged down by Nikki's indiscretions.

He deserves better.

The next morning, Nikki focused on preparing for her appointment with the North Louisiana Teachers' Union. She arrived early and accepted an offer of coffee. The office sat in one of the shabbier areas of town, although it appeared to be well staffed from all the activity.

"Florence Dunn," the energetic woman said, extending her arm.

"Nicole Dayton." Nikki shook her hand.

Once inside Dunn's office, Nikki told her the whole story. Dunn seemed more fascinated with the book than anything else.

"So, they terminated you on the same day you brought

them evidence of sexual harassment? That's insane. You have a case."

"I do?"

Florence rolled her eyes. "Of course. Someone leaves a sexually suggestive book in your mailbox, and later the same day they turn around and fire you? That's like punishing the whistleblower."

"But the student and I—"

"You had a prior relationship. End of story. You knew one another from college."

"Shouldn't I have disclosed that?"

"You made an error in judgment." Florence paused. "Wait a minute, didn't you say you didn't know he was a student at Grayson when you accepted the position?"

"That's right."

"Okay, even better. You had no idea he was a student at Grayson, so you didn't need to disclose it to the college or the school. The only thing you can admit to is an error in judgment in not disclosing it *after* you started student teaching."

"Okay."

"But look. You're both adults. This isn't Texas. There is nothing illegal about dating an adult student. Might be questionable, but not illegal."

"But back to the book—"

"Yeah. You gotta call them on that. They did nothing to protect you from someone who fostered a hostile work environment." Florence pressed a button on her phone. "Lacy, get in here!"

Nikki wondered who Lacy could be but didn't have to

wonder for long. The door opened, and a young pixie-faced woman walked in.

"Lacy, this is Nicole Dayton. Sit in on this. We're gonna set up a meeting at Grayson High, and if I can't make it, you're going in my place." Florence scanned some sheets of paper tacked on to a corkboard above her desk. "Ramos is still the principal?" She dialed a number.

"Yes." Nikki was impressed how fast Dunn moved into action.

"This is Florence Dunn from the North Louisiana Teachers' Union. May I speak with Mrs. Ramos please?"

Initially, the school refused to meet with them, saying it was a closed case. When Dunn threatened legal action, they relented. Mrs. Ramos promised to call back with a meeting time, and she did. It was scheduled for the next morning, Friday, at eight thirty.

Another text from Isaach: *Call me. I care about you and want to talk to you.*

Nikki struggled with uncertainty. There wasn't much she could say to him now. She wanted to know he was okay, but she'd probably messed up his life. The school could expel him and it would all be her fault. Shame prevented her from picking up the phone and calling him.

Isaach had set her on fire and led her across new thresholds of pleasure. He'd brought her to climax after climax and heightened her passion. When she was with him, the levels of satisfaction kept going up a step. She wanted Isaach and he wanted her and it would be criminal to be kept apart.

They both had so much on the line. Fighting for herself would be fighting for Isaach as well. If she could be cleared of any wrongdoing, that would clear him as well.

But I did do wrong.

Getting involved with a student was sheer stupidity. Nikki had let her guard down one time too many with Isaach on the grounds of Grayson High. She would fight to stay at Arcadia, but she had to admit she had screwed up big-time at Grayson.

She wasn't sure what would come out of tomorrow morning's meeting. Dunn came across like a barracuda, which could be either good or bad. Then again, she needed someone like Dunn to get her out of this mess. She was so distraught over being canned she had forgotten about the book until she'd met with Barbara. Maybe that was her trump card.

I should call Isaach.

Back at her dorm room, changed for work, she grabbed her phone and hit his number before she lost her nerve. Isaach answered on the second ring.

"How are you, Nikki?"

"Okay. Sorry I haven't been in touch. Isaach, I'm sorry. I feel awful."

"It's all my fault, Nikki. I never shoulda done what I did. I feel terrible and I don't know what to do."

"What do you mean?"

"Your degree depended on this gig."

"A gig. Not this gig. I have a meeting with Mrs. Ramos tomorrow. The teachers' union set it up."

"So you think there's a chance?"

"There's gotta be or else the teachers' union wouldn't be wasting their time with me. I'm not even a member."

"Straight up. I want to see you, Nikki."

"I want to see you, too. Let's see what happens after tomorrow's meeting. I'm too exhausted and stressed out to even think now."

"I respect that."

"Isaach, it's not your fault. Don't blame yourself. I should have practiced discretion. It's part of my code of conduct or whatever they call it."

"Damn, Nikki, you didn't do anything wrong. I'm the one who can't keep my hands off you."

Nikki smiled. A tingling ran through her belly, knowing he wanted her.

"I'll let you know what happens."

"Okay. Be good."

Nikki put the phone down. She was on the verge of losing everything. Or was she? Isaach still seemed interested, but would he be without her presence to titillate him five days a week? Would his parents accept that he'd romanced a common, low class piece of trailer park trash?

Dammit.

She had to stop thinking that way. She'd accomplished so much since her youth, such as clawing her way out of the gutter to work as many hours per week as she could, saving to buy her own car, and saving to pay room and board on top of tuition.

That's one thing Isaach likes about me.

It took a while for Nikki to realize it, but Isaach admired her independence. He really had none of his own. Sure, he came and went as he pleased. But he depended on his parents for room, board, gasoline, and just about everything else.

She'd been so wrapped up in her own long days she hadn't really helped him as much as she could. He was a senior, poised to graduate this year. She should have been guiding him through job applications, stuff that he really needed or at least wanted. As his teacher, she should have been more of a mentor.

Should is an ugly word.

It implied regret and loss. She needed to focus on moving forward and not agonizing over should this or should that. That bachelor's degree would hang on her wall no matter what she had to do to get it. No small town backwards ass school like Grayson High could stop her. She grabbed her bag and headed to the restaurant.

The next morning, she arrived at the campus of Grayson High School at eight fifteen. The receptionist gave her an odd look and mumbled something into her two-way radio.

"I have an eight thirty appointment with Mrs. Ramos."

"Just a minute," the receptionist said.

Within minutes, Mr. Da'Trin appeared. "Come with me, Miss Dayton."

Nikki didn't like the way this was going already. "I have an appointment."

"I know. Right this way."

Da'Trin led her into a small room. Much too small to be a meeting room.

"Why are we here?"

"Sit down, please." Da'Trin took a seat.

Nikki reluctantly sat opposite him. "So?"

"Miss Dayton, when someone has been relieved of their duties at Grayson, or anywhere in Portsmith ISD I should say, you can't come back on campus."

"I said I have an appointment."

"I know, but you can't be in a place visible to the other staff and students."

Nikki did notice the room had no windows, nor did the door. "You're for real?"

"It's Portsmith ISD policies and procedures."

"Oh, really? I would love to see that in writing."

Da'Trin went silent.

"I didn't think so," Nikki said.

Da'Trin leaned forward, his arms resting on his thighs. "I know it might not make any difference to you at this point, but I didn't say anything to Mrs. Ramos that reflected badly on you."

Nikki's gazed roved up and down him. "You're right. I couldn't care less."

"You know, Miss Dayton, now that you're not working here—"

"Da'Trin, I don't need to hear another word out of you. Please don't waste your breath."

His face tightened and he nodded. After a few awkward minutes, his two-way radio crackled and he gestured for her to follow him.

Da'Trin led her into a large conference room. Miss Dunn

and a gentleman she didn't recognize were there. Also, Mrs. Ramos, and a couple of others she didn't know.

"Good morning," Dunn greeted her.

"Good morning," Nikki murmured and had a seat by Dunn.

"Thank you, Mr. Da'Trin. You can wait outside. I'll call you if I need you. I'm Claudia Ramos, the principal at Grayson High," she said to Dunn. "To my right is my supervisor, Leona Page, director of school performance. To her right is Alberta Wayne, investigations."

Mrs. Ramos gestured to Miss Dunn.

"I'm Florence Dunn, president of the North Louisiana Teachers' Union. With me is Nicole Dayton, student at Arcadia College, and Nigel Warren, union attorney."

Mrs. Ramos nodded. "This week, Miss Dayton was terminated as a student teacher."

"Excuse me," Florence said. "Excuse me for interrupting you, Mrs. Ramos, but we don't want to take up more of your time than we have to. That's not the issue at hand today." She turned to Nikki. "The book."

Nikki removed the book from her handbag and handed it to Dunn.

"This is why we're here." Dunn placed the book on the table so Mrs. Ramos and her team could see it. "The book has a sexually suggestive title as well as racial insensitivity."

Page and Wayne looked at the book.

"Mrs. Ramos, what was done to investigate the hostile work environment that was fostered when this book was placed in Nicole Dayton's mailbox?"

Mrs. Ramos appeared uncomfortable. "Nothing," she said.

"Nothing," Dunn repeated. "The book before you ladies is a tangible piece of evidence. I can see by your faces that it's making you uncomfortable looking at it. How do you think Nicole Dayton felt? She had a prior relationship with an African-American man she met on the campus of Arcadia College."

Page and Wayne exchanged glances.

"That's right, ladies. She felt far more uncomfortable than you're feeling now. Yet Grayson High School did nothing. No investigation. Nothing to protect Miss Dayton from a hostile work environment."

"There wasn't any time—"

"Excuse me, Mrs. Ramos, for interrupting you again. There was time to dismiss Nicole upon *suspicions* of inappropriate conduct. Is this book a suspicion, ma'am?"

Mrs. Ramos shook her head.

Mrs. Page turned to Nikki. "When did you find the book in your mailbox?"

"Wednesday morning."

"Nothing was done about it on Wednesday." Florence Dunn was on a roll, hammering away at Mrs. Ramos. Nikki wondered why she bothered to bring an attorney since she was doing all the talking. "But the same day, Miss Dayton was terminated. She received a call that same day from her college advisor. Terminated based on mere suspicion."

Mrs. Wayne spoke up. "We have the testimony of an eyewitness—"

"A biased one, Alberta. The girl was a jilted ex-girlfriend of the young man. All we know is that Miss Dayton and the young man were in the library at the same time. There is no impartial witness who saw anything to back up the teenage girl's testimony, is there?"

"No," Mrs. Wayne said.

"Do you see the injustice in firing Nicole Dayton based on suspicion when you did nothing to investigate the harassment against her?"

The ladies glanced at one another. Mrs. Ramos cleared her throat. "Miss Dunn, we cannot reinstate Miss Dayton to her position here."

"We're not asking you to."

Nikki shot a glance at Dunn.

We're not?

Dunn continued. "All we ask is that you contact Arcadia College and withdraw your complaint. Tell them it was a misunderstanding, and you have no evidence whatsoever that there was any wrongdoing on the part of Nicole Dayton."

Mrs. Ramos looked at the other two ladies, then down at her notes. "Miss Dunn, would you excuse the three of us for a moment?"

"Certainly."

Mrs. Ramos gestured for Page and Wayne to follow her out of the room.

CHAPTER TWENTY

Nikki had to admit, she was impressed with Dunn's style. Her razor-sharp responses hadn't left much for those other ladies to say. If anyone could get her out of this mess, it was Dunn.

"I gotta hand it to you, Dunn." Nigel finally spoke up. "You did it again."

"You think it'll go our way?"

Nigel nodded. "Yes. They seem to have overreached on this one. I can understand their concerns about suspicions between a student and teacher, regardless of the fact they're both adults, but there's no evidence."

Nikki sat in that uncomfortable chair for a long time. Ramos and her cohorts were not making their wait brief.

Mr. Da'Trin stuck his head into the door. "Can I get any of you something to drink?"

"No, thanks," Florence said.

Nikki shook her head. Da'Trin winked at her.

He's gotta be kidding.

Florence chatted with Nigel while Nikki grew impatient.

Her thoughts drifted to Isaach and how much she wanted to see him again. Perhaps it would be best if she was not allowed to return to Grayson.

After what seemed like an eternity, Mrs. Ramos returned to the room. Mrs. Wayne and Mrs. Page accompanied her.

"I apologize to have kept you waiting so long. We had a lot to consider, and we've notified Arcadia College that our investigation concluded no evidence of wrongdoing on the part of Nicole Dayton." Nikki noticed Mrs. Ramos was reading from a prepared statement. "We regret that Miss Dayton cannot return to Grayson High School but have informed Arcadia College there is no reason Miss Dayton cannot continue her student teaching assignment elsewhere. Arcadia College has agreed to assist in finding a suitable job site and will give Miss Dayton continuous credit."

Mrs. Ramos looked up from her notes. "What that means, Miss Dayton, is that your student teaching credit will be continuous throughout the rest of the semester. You will not be penalized for the time off between your assignment here and however long it takes to place you at another school."

Nikki nodded.

"Thank you, ladies," Miss Dunn said as she reached for the paperback book on the table and handed it to Nikki. "We'll look forward to hearing the results of your investigation on the book." There was a huge grin on Dunn's face.

Nikki figured Dunn was being sarcastic. It was a closed matter as far as Nikki was concerned. She knew the school wasn't going to do a damn thing about the book, and at this point, she didn't care.

**

Saturday, north Louisiana was hot and dry, a perfect day to be outdoors. Nikki had pulled a shift last night at the restaurant but took today off. As much as she needed the money, she also needed a breather.

Isaach picked her up at the dorm and drove her to a park in a small town between Arcadia and Portsmith. Nikki brought along food and cold drinks. The air smelled of flowers blooming. They spread out a blanket under a large magnolia tree. She rested her head against his chest and closed her eyes.

"How do you feel?" Isaach asked.

"Peaceful, finally."

"What will you do?"

"I'll find another gig. I made some inquiries on my own, plus my advisor is helping me."

She kept her eyes shut and enjoyed the moment. His lean, muscular arms held her close to him, and she relished the calmness. The stress from the week slowly withered away as she smelled the freshly laundered fabric of his shirt. She wanted to taste him and leaned her head up to his neck, gently brushing lips against his throat.

He shifted position and placed his lips against hers. She welcomed his kisses and hungered for more. But for now, she enjoyed his taste. Nothing mattered right now except being in his arms and feeling his tongue explore her mouth.

She inhaled the scent of magnolia and savored the warmth of this perfect day. She leaned back and looked at Isaach, his beautiful chocolate complexion and almond eyes.

"Oh, did I tell you? I filled out some job applications."

"Where?"

"Online. Local stuff." Isaach grinned.

"Good luck with that."

"Hey, you wanna meet my parents tomorrow?" He raised his brow.

"Are you serious?"

Isaach nodded.

"Don't they know about what happened?"

"At the high school? Naw."

"Are you sure?"

"Yeah. They're having some people over. I thought it might be a good time. No pressure. Just drop in, have something to eat, bounce."

"Okay." Nikki wasn't sure. She said okay because he asked, but she was apprehensive. If they were both busy, perhaps they didn't hear or pay attention to local gossip.

He wants me to meet his parents.

She reached up to take his face in her hands and kissed him again. He slid his body over hers and she felt a wave of heat rush through her. Lying on this blanket in the beautiful end-of-summer heat, she counted her blessings. She was on track in her career, or at least soon would be, and had found a man who cared for her.

Perhaps this was finally the time to ease away from the nonstop workaholic lifestyle she'd been leading and enjoy the pleasures of Isaach's attention. The day she had turned down that extra shift at the restaurant in favor of seeing him was the day she knew she was hooked.

"Are you hungry?"

"Always," he said.

"I brought along a lot of stuff I picked up fresh at the deli this morning. And plenty to drink."

He kissed her. "Thank you." He sat up and wrapped his hands around his knees.

"What's wrong?"

"I won't be able to rest until you're teaching again. I still can't shake the fact it's my fault you're not at Grayson."

"Isaach, neither one of us is any more at fault than the other. We got out of hand. We need to move on from that."

"I just want you to succeed."

"I will. It may take some time to get another gig, but I'll do it."

She placed her hand on his back and rubbed slowly and in a circular motion. He stretched out so he reclined on his back and pulled Nikki on top of him. A gentle summer breeze blew through her mane of red hair. He kissed her like there was no tomorrow.

She needed his encouragement. The years of struggling had taken their toll. Everything had been work and school. She hadn't really built a support system. Even Carla, whom she considered a friend as well as a roommate, was seldom there. Isaach, in the short time she'd known him, had reached out to her and extended himself whenever needed.

His passion ignited her dormant fuse. Whenever she

spent time with him, their connection deepened. She marveled at the heights he'd taken her to and longed for more challenges. She'd experienced more desire with him than with anyone before him, not that there were many.

Later, after a healthy spoonful of potato salad and other picnic foods, they strolled by the lake. The park was grand and well maintained, the pride and joy of a small town. As they held hands away from the college and the high school, she was filled with freedom and recklessness. Being with him made it so easy for anything else to just melt away.

"Any ideas where you might teach?"

"Around here, hopefully. I got sent to Portsmith ISD because everything around here was filled, but you never know. Opportunities could open at any time."

"I want to see you on the weekends. Even during the week if you have a night off."

"I want to see you, too," Nikki said. "But that's an awful lot to spend on gas."

"No more than you were spending driving to Centerdale every day."

"True."

He led her under a tree, where they would have some shade. They sat on a bench and watched the ducks moving to and fro in the water.

"Something I've been meaning to ask you."

"Go ahead."

"How did you get the complaint dropped?"

She had feared he would ask, but she needed to be honest. "Kind of a long story. I went to see an attorney I knew, she sent me to the teachers' union, and they set up a meeting with Ramos."

"That doesn't sound like a very long story."

"Do you know I've never seen you play basketball?"

"You just changed the subject." He gave her a look that indicated he wasn't in the mood for games.

"Someone left a book in my mailbox at Grayson High."

"What about it?"

"The book was very sexual and the teachers' union used that as a wedge to get the complaint against me dismissed. The president of the union argued that the book was a form of harassment and the school didn't properly investigate."

"So why not come back to Grayson?"

"I can't for a number of reasons. It might not be best. They can't completely ignore the other claim. They just withdrew the complaint from the college. In other words, I'm done at Grayson, but I still can remain enrolled at Arcadia. I won't be brought before a disciplinary board or whatever."

"Got it. What was the book?"

"It's in my dorm room. I'll show it to you later."

Nikki got up and wandered to the edge of the lake. She took some bread out of her basket and tossed it to the ducks. They pounced on it like cats on mice. She hoped by the time they got back to her room he would forget about the book. It wasn't important anymore, and she didn't want him embarking on a mission to hunt down whoever had left it.

His arms slipped around her waist, and ripples of excitement ran through her. She'd been so lost in thought she hadn't heard him slide behind her. He held her while she tossed the remaining bits of bread to the ducks and her optimism returned. She had everything she needed to succeed. Her place at Arcadia was secured; she had an income and the support of a good man.

Isaach had proven many times he'd be there for her, and she was grateful for his words of encouragement. One of his hands slid up to her hair and he brushed it away from her shoulder. Her body shivered. His lips pressed against her neck, and warmth surged through her. Nikki closed her eyes, savoring the gorgeous Louisiana summer day and her sensual Louisiana man. As the heat spread through her body, she held on to his forearm wrapped around her and knew she was where she wanted to be. She had found the man of her dreams and nothing would stop them from soaring together.

If you enjoyed Isaach and Nikki's story, please consider leaving a review on the retail site where you purchased it, or on Goodreads.

Isaach and Nikki also appear in the novelette, *A Thanksgiving Gift*, which appears in the novel-length volume *Early Finishers*.

About the author

Jamie Jones writes interracial romance. Jamie spent nine years working as a public school teacher, and that provided the backdrop of Jamie's debut series, The Tempted Teachers Series. *Lesson Plans, Guided Practice,* and *Explicit Instruction* all take place within the framework of the public education system.

Now, Jamie is excited to introduce a new series: The Bennett Family Series. Jamie lives in Austin, Texas....where people are nice.

Visit my website at jamiejonesauthor.com

Also by Jamie Jones

The Tempted Teachers Series

novels
LESSON PLANS (Book 1)
GUIDED PRACTICE (Book 2)
EXPLICIT INSTRUCTION (Book 3)

novellas
RESPONSE TO INTERVENTION (Book 4)
COMMON CORE (Book 5)
PROFESSIONAL DEVELOPMENT (Book 6)
BELL RINGERS (Books 4-6 in one volume)

novelettes
A HALLOWEEN TREAT
A HALLOWEEN TRICK
A CHRISTMAS HONEYMOON
A CHRISTMAS ANNIVERSARY
COMMON CORE: SUMMER SCHOOL
A THANKSGIVING GIFT
EARLY FINISHERS (all six novelettes in one volume)

The Bennett Family Series

Here is a brief excerpt from
Response to Intervention

When Carolyn was told her job depended on getting up the reading scores of at-risk kids, she figured she'd be getting something more up in the process. Lester City Elementary School sat on the other side of the tracks. The kids were poor, and the resources available to teachers were poorer.

"Do a good job for us, Miss Carmichael, and we may offer you a permanent position here." The personnel director had one of the biggest shit-eating grins she'd ever seen.

Carolyn accepted the job with the dubious title of Reading Interventionist. Fresh out of grad school, Carolyn knew what an interventionist did, but she also realized there was more than one way to do it. She had to come up with her own strategies to get the reading scores up. She had come up with a few in college, but she wanted to tailor her strategies to the individual needs of the students.

"It's all about Dibels, Miss Carmichael."

"Dibels *Next*," Carolyn said with the most saccharine smile she could muster. Dibels Next was an assessment tool administered three times a year to progress-monitor the reading level of school children, and Carolyn administered several as part of the field experience for her master's degree.

"You know your stuff, Miss Carmichael." The personnel director, Miss Paradise, walked Carolyn to the door, and Carolyn couldn't help but marvel at how Miss Paradise teeter-tottered on three inch heels.

"I'll do a good job for you, Miss Paradise."

"I'm sure you will," Paradise said, her plump face red from the wine she probably drank as her lunch.

The next morning, Carolyn rose and shone early to head across the tracks to Lester City Elementary School. She had to admit, she'd never been on that side of town before. This part of Louisiana was all about the haves and the have-nots. Carolyn had always lived firmly in the haves. Her family could afford to send her to college and grad school. She hoped her career made it all worth it.

"Teachers don't get paid much," her mother had told her. "But they make it back in satisfaction."

Yeah, right.

The only satisfaction Carolyn needed right now was a paycheck. She decided to go conservative on her first day. White blouse, black skirt, and ten-inch heels. No, not really. Six inches would do. After all, she was only five foot two and needed the help.

Dammit. I'm lost.

Carolyn had to get to work on time as she didn't want to be late her first day. Miss Paradise would lose all faith in her, and she still had to meet her principal. She drove over the bridge and crossed the tracks. At least she was on the right side of Lester City; now all she had to do was find the damn school.

She pulled her car over when she observed a man sweeping puddles of rainwater along his walkway.

"Hey, do you know where Lester City is?"

"You're in Lester City," the man said.

This man thinks I'm an idiot.

"I mean the school."

"Elementary?"

"Yes."

"Turn left and you'll see it."

"Thanks."

Carolyn turned left, and sure enough, there it was. Lester City Elementary School. Home of the reading scores that *sucked* according to the brass at central office. The school was one of those institutional looking rows of cellblocks masquerading as classrooms. Then again, all schools built in the fifties looked like that. The place had to be sixty years old if it was a day.

She squeezed her Buick in a spot for a compact, and then strutted her way up to the main office. The school smelled of bleach. The windows were dirty, always a bad sign. If they didn't keep the windows clean, she was almost afraid to see the classrooms. It was thankfully still early, and Carolyn always liked to be prompt. She clutched her briefcase in one hand; her sweater slung over the other arm, and found the office.

The office smells worse than the breezeway.

"Good morning." Carolyn said to the receptionist.

The old woman seemed burdened to look up from her newspaper. "Yes?"

"I'm Carolyn Carmichael, Reading Interventionist."

The old woman scowled. She pressed a button on her phone. "Mizz Shelton. Some new teacher here." Her gaze dropped back down to her newspaper.

The main door opened, and the most beautiful specimen of black manhood walked through the door. He had on an institutional uniform, with his name embroidered on a patch. *DaShon*. He had sparkling brown eyes and a smile worthy of a Trident commercial.

"Miss Mason, there's a damn Buick out there sticking its ass out so far the busses can barely get by."

Carolyn blushed. "That's my car."

"Oh, I am so sorry, miss. No disrespect intended. Would you kindly move your vehicle to the rear parking lot so the busses don't hit it?"

"Sure, if you can show me where the rear parking lot is." Carolyn wanted him to show her a lot more.

"Right this way." DaShon smiled and gestured toward the door.

Once outside, Carolyn turned to the gorgeous young man. "Carolyn Carmichael." She held out her hand.

"DaShon Turner. Pleased to meet you." He had curly black hair, a scruffy face, and sparkling studs in his ears. He was tall, although it didn't take much to be taller than her. His handshake was firm, and he had charm and charisma that could melt an iceberg.

"How long have you worked here, DaShon?"

"I'm actually a temp custodian filling in for the regular assistant who's on a leave of absence. Been here a couple of months. You?"

"Today's my fist day."

"Yeah, I figured that out, princess. Doing what?"

"Reading Interventionist."

DaShon sighed. "They need all the help they can get."

Carolyn led him to her car, and she was astonished to see him hop into the passenger seat.

"You want me to show you where it is, don't you?" He grinned.

Carolyn was going to say something smart but relented. "Sure."

When he buckled his seatbelt, she noticed his large hairy arms and became moist between her legs. If there was anything she couldn't resist, it was a hairy man. His deep, rich caramel skin only made him hotter.

"Okay, back out here. Now hang to your right. Go to the end of the drive and turn right."

"I appreciate your directions."

"Okay, now go straight ahead all the way back. Past the library and hang another right. There you are."

"Crap." Carolyn didn't mean to say that.

"What's wrong?"

"You call this a parking lot?" It was basically mud.

"Well, the school does. I don't. Pull up here."

Carolyn did as she was instructed.

"Wait here," DaShon told her.

She obediently waited as he hopped out of the car and came around to her side. He gestured for her to open the door, so she did so.

"Okay, step out carefully. Just your legs. Don't put your

255

feet on the ground. Now scoot up in your seat. That's it." DaShon scooped her up in his arms and carried her through the mud.

"What the—"

"Yeah, keep complaining and I'll drop you." DaShon laughed.

Carolyn kept quiet. He was right and had saved her from a big mess. Once safely back on the concrete, he set her down.

"Hey, thanks, but…"

"What?"

"I need my sweater and briefcase."

"Not a problem." DaShon traced his steps back through the mud and retrieved her items. "Here you go, madame."

"It's mademoiselle, if you know the difference."

"I'm blessed that I do." DaShon sauntered away. "Have a good day, teach!"

Carolyn simmered in more ways than one. He could have walked her back to the office, not that she couldn't find her own way, but she was also flushed from head to toe from his humongous sex appeal. The man was hot as hell. In her car, she almost forgot she was at a school. All he had to do was make a move, and she would have swooned right then and there on the front seat.

The principal!

www.ingramcontent.com/pod-product-compliance
Lightning Source LLC
Chambersburg PA
CBHW070908180626
46817CB00003B/968